FLY CATCHING & *Other Bits & Pieces*

SUSAN P. BAKER

Fly Catching
And Other Bits & Pieces

ISBN-13: 978-0-9980390-2-2

This book is memoir. It reflects the author's present recollections of experiences over time. Some names and characteristics have been changed, some events have been compressed, and some dialogue has been recreated.

Interior formatting & cover design by Laurie Barboza @ Design Stash Books. DesignStashBooks@gmail.com

Produced in the United States of America.

For information and/or permission to use excerpts, contact:

Refugio Press
P.O. Box 3937
Galveston, TX 77552.

BOOKS BY SUSAN P. BAKER

NOVELS:

My First Murder, No. 1 in the Mavis Davis Mystery Series
P.I. Mavis uncovers corruption deep in the heart of Texas while searching for the murderer of a mysterious woman.

The Sweet Scent of Murder, No. 2 in the Mavis Davis Mystery Series
When her search for a missing teenager turns to murder, Mavis discovers disgusting details about a Houston River Oaks' family.

Murder and Madness, No. 3 in the Mavis Davis Mystery Series
To fulfill a dying woman's wish, Mavis plunges headfirst into the Galveston island investigation of a grisly ax murder.

Death of a Prince, No. 1 in the Lady Lawyer Series
Mother & daughter criminal defense lawyers defend the alleged murderer of a millionaire plaintiffs' attorney in Galveston, Texas.

Death of a Rancher's Daughter, No. 2 in the Lady Lawyer Series
Lawyers Sandra and Erma battle prejudice against wrongfully accused Latina defendant in murder trial in Texas Hill Country.

Ledbetter Street, A Novel of Second Chances
With the deck stacked against her, a Galveston mother fights the court system for guardianship of her autistic son.

Suggestion of Death
A father who can't pay his child support investigates the mysterious deaths of deadbeat dads in the Texas Hill Country.

Texas Style Justice
Faced with life altering decisions, an ambitious Texas Hill Country judge must determine what price she is willing to pay to reach her ultimate goal of being appointed to the Supreme Court.

UNAWARE, A Suspense Novel
Galveston, Texas Attorney Dena Armstrong is about to break out from under the two controlling men in her life, unaware that a stranger has other plans for her.

NONFICTION:

Heart of Divorce Advice from a Judge
Divorce advice especially for those who are considering representing themselves.

Murdered Judges of the 20th Century
True Stories of Judges Killed in America.

WWW.SUSANPBAKER.COM

DEDICATION

For Caleb, our basketball lover

CONTENTS

INTRODUCTION.. ix

FLY CATCHING...1

PAPER, SCISSORS, ROCK 5

OUR GOOD SAMARITAN 9

QUEEN FOR A DAY 17

MY RUDE AWAKENING 23

THE DARK CHILD...29

I DIDN'T BURN THE HOUSE DOWN...................43

NINA 51

A STATE OF TORMENT..................................59

A LITTLE GIFT FROM HEAVEN........................71

THE RULES 91

NEXT TIME.. 115

THE NOT SO GREAT COOKIE CAPER................ 123

BYGONES 129

DOUBLE OR NOTHING.............................. 145

JURY DUTY 155

LETTER TO CHARLIE 161

RETRIBUTION.. 167

MISS EDNA... 169

WHY DO THEY STAY? A RHETORICAL QUESTION .. 181

SHADES OF GRAY 195

THANK YOU FOR READING!........................ 199

ACKNOWLEDGEMENTS 201

ABOUT THE AUTHOR............................... 203

INTRODUCTION

This book is a collection of short pieces I wrote over the years, some dating back too long ago to remember. As I grew older and my parents passed away, I realized my own mortality. A day would come when my children would be cleaning out my office—my house—and more than likely pitch most of my writings and writing paraphernalia. I hated to think these pieces would be thrown away.

I remember a conversation that took place between one of my daughters and myself twenty-plus years ago after I'd married for the second time. Having to combine two households into one caused me to have to dispose of some of my possessions. I asked her if she'd like to come down and go through my photographs and take what she wanted. She said no. She'd just wait until I was dead.

I've given that conversation a lot of thought. A collection in a book is much easier to keep and pass down than boxes of printed matter or disks that fit no computer that isn't in a museum.

Most of these pieces haven't been seen before. They vary between memoir/autobiographical, nonfiction, and fiction. Some are fun. Some are sad. Some may make the reader angry. Some show my dark side. Most readers will have an emotional reaction to some of them. At the least, my descendants will get a clearer picture of who I am/was and what passed through my imagination.

Autobiographical/memoir

FLY CATCHING

My mama tried to instill in her four kids the value of a penny. When we turned six, she awarded us a quarter allowance with the promise of a nickel raise each birthday. So long as we had done our chores, Mama would dole out our stipend on Saturday mornings before we all traipsed into town to the new grocery store.

I would buy three chocolate-covered donuts for ten cents, a "funny" book for another dime, and have a few pennies left over for the gumball machine. I could earn more money for work around the house, but the jobs for my age group were limited.

We lived on Offatts Bayou on a large, low-lying lot full of salt cedars. We owned chickens, geese, always at least one cat and dog, and once, a donkey. In good weather, we'd swim, play, and fish. We'd bring Mama the crabs and fish as we caught them, wiping the mud off our bare feet before entering the kitchen, dumping our catch into the sink. The spicy aroma of crab boil often hung in the air like a heavy cloud along with the fishy smell of ocean water.

I can still hear Mama hollering, "Don't hold the screen door open! You're letting in the flies!" The banging door behind us would echo as we laughed and ran back to the pier. Mama didn't pay us for what we caught, except for the flies. There were always lots of flies. My five-year-old, tow-headed brother and I were usually the ones desperate enough to engage in fly catching. We fought over a long-handled flyswatter that looked like a mesh hotcake turner. The loser got the default weapon, a rolled-up newspaper.

We would pile our dead flies on separate corners of the dining table so there would be no confusion over which carcasses belonged to whom. We had to keep an eye on them, too, so the ones that were only injured didn't get up and crawl away.

The most difficult part of our job was not smashing a fly too hard. If body parts were incapable of identification, Mama would not pay us. We hated to be falsely accused of fraud. If we did squash one too flat, we would scrape up the sticky body parts and set them away from the rest so she could see we were being above-board.

We usually cashed in when we had twenty-five very dead flies. Mama didn't like to see any wiggling. Regardless of the number, if suppertime rolled around, she would arrive for the count, pay us a penny for every five flies, and make us dump the entire catch into the trash.

Now, over sixty years later, when I find pennies and pick them up, I remember the 1950s and catching flies on the Galveston bayou.

Years ago I took a nonfiction writing class where the instructor placed various objects before us and asked us to write a story inspired by them. The events depicted below are true, though one name is changed.

PAPER, SCISSORS, ROCK

"I don't want to play with you. You hit too hard," I told my big brother.

"Come on, Sue, I won't hit you hard today. I promise."

"That's what you said the last time. It took two weeks for the bruise to go away."

But he assured me that he really meant it, that I could trust him, that he was my brother and wouldn't lie to me. He took my hand in his and as he swiped two fingers across my wrist, he said, "I won't hit you any harder than that, like a piece of paper scraping across your skin. Besides, you might win today."

Paper, scissors, rock. Paper, scissors, rock. Paper, scissors, rock. Whack.

When I was little, we had cousins who came to live with us when their families fell on hard times. One, who was six years my senior, wanted to be a beautician and would practice on me. She would brush my long dark hair into smooth ponytails, something I had a hard time doing. When she pulled out her scissors though, I drew the line. "You can't cut my hair," I said. "Only Mrs. Deeds is allowed to cut my hair."

"But I can save Aunt Jean a lot of money. All I'm going to do is give you a little trim on the ends and cut your bangs. I need the practice." I let her do it. She was, after all, really good at making ponytails. And when she cut her own hair, it looked like a pixie's. She snipped off the dead ends. That worked okay. But, after she cut my bangs, when she moved away from in front of the mirror, I discovered the reason she needed practice.

"Ride the Ferris wheel with me," my big sister said.

"No. You always rock it when it stops on top. I don't like that. It scares me. I'm afraid I'll fall out."

"Oh," she coaxed, "I won't rock it this time. I promise. Mama says I can't ride it alone. If you don't ride it with me, I won't get to ride it at all, and I want to so badly."

"Okay, if you really promise." I was happy to know that I didn't have to worry about her rocking it anymore. We got in line at the ticket booth, purchased our tickets, and climbed into the seat held steady by the attendant. My chest felt hollow as the wheel rose into the air and floated down, rose into the air and floated down. It was going to be all right. I sighed. Sat back, but continued to hold on tight. Then the wheel slowed to a halt. Our chair stopped on top. My sister leaned forward and laughed. She rocked backward and forward, and my heart fell out, flopping over and over until it hit the ground.

Years later, right before I got my divorce, my husband said my problem was that I was suspicious of everybody. I agreed with him and considered challenging him to a game of Paper, Scissors, Rock.

My father came from a poor family of ten children and rose to be a district court judge. He was a good -hearted person who was known, before he took the bench, as the poor man's lawyer of Galveston. This is a barely-fictionalized version of what life was like for my family with him at the bow. (A version of this story by the title Learning Lessons appeared in Tidelines II, An Anthology of Galveston Writers, Galveston Writers Coalition 1999.)

OUR GOOD SAMARITAN

"Da-ddeeeee," the little brown-haired girl wailed from where she sat in the middle seat of the 1957 Ford station wagon. "Don't stop. Please don't stop. *Walt Disney* comes on at six."

Watching out the side window as they were returning from their Sunday afternoon drive, the youngest daughter in the family had been silently praying they wouldn't come upon another car that had gotten stuck in the sand. She cried out now as she saw the car with a woman and children standing beside it. The man was behind the steering wheel with the driver's door hanging open. One of the rear tires spun in the dry, powdery beach sand.

She hadn't quite given Daddy time to see the stranded family before she'd cried out, but it didn't matter anyhow. She knew he would find them as if by instinct. No one in need escaped Daddy's attention; no one.

Feeling their slowly moving vehicle easing to a halt, eight-year-old Sara squeezed her eyes shut as her father exclaimed that he'd spotted someone stuck again. They had to stop and render aid. They couldn't leave those poor folks with their sunburned children to wait until somebody else came along.

"La, la, la, la, la," the girl sang half to herself as she stuck her fingers in her ears and closed her eyes. She didn't want to hear what Daddy said. The last half of *Old Yeller* was coming on tonight, and she couldn't bear to miss it.

The station wagon came to a complete stop, and the weight of Daddy left the car. She peeked through her eyelashes as Daddy approached the man behind the steering wheel.

"Mama," she cried, reaching toward the front seat with a sense of desperation. "Are we going to be stuck here for hours again?"

Mama twisted around in the front seat and faced the children. "You know how your father is, dear," she said with a sigh and a shake of her head.

There was nothing for Sara to do but watch out the window and pray that after Daddy helped these people, he wouldn't find anyone else all the way home.

Daddy had always been like that. Ever since she was little, she could remember Daddy helping people. He'd help old people with their bags. He'd help poor people. She heard Mama and him talking about it. He worked for poor people, she'd heard him say. They couldn't afford to pay him.

Sundays were special days. The family went to church together, and afterward Daddy would fry chicken. Sundays were the only days she saw her daddy much. Sometimes he'd stop frying their chicken and go get poor people out of jail. Mama would have to finish cooking. The phone was always ringing, and Daddy was always telling them he'd be right there. Sometimes the phone rang in the middle of the night, and Sara would hear him leave.

Daddy helped other people, too. When her family was out in their cabin-cruiser, Daddy would tow people's broken-down boats home. And animals. Daddy liked animals. She always knew if she brought a kitty home while Daddy was there, she'd get to keep it. Daddy liked everybody. What did they call a person like Daddy? She would have to think about it. She was too mad right now. She just wanted to see *Old Yeller* on television that night.

Later that summer of '58, after she had turned nine, Sara and her parents, two brothers, and sister, were all piled in the station wagon, approaching the Bolivar Peninsula from the east. As they came around the bend, they spotted the seemingly endless line of cars waiting to board the ferry that would carry them across the bay to Galveston. Almost in unison, a groan spilled out of each child.

"We're almost home," Daddy's cheerful voice came back to them. "A little while longer won't hurt. Just enjoy the fresh air and the smell of the gulf."

It was the very last day of their annual August vacation. Tomorrow, Daddy would have to go back to work. She'd heard Mama and Daddy talking. This year, money was tight, so the six of them had gone camping all the way to Florida and back for two whole weeks. They'd been to Pensacola, Miami, and Key West. Sara'd had a good time, but, as Mama would say, she was ready to be home in her own bed.

Sara was tired of fighting with her sister every time a knee or elbow crossed over the imaginary line that divided the seat in half, and the way the boys pulled her ponytail when Mama wasn't looking made Sara mad. Mama thought she was making it up, but they really did pull her hair. They thought it was funny that they never got caught. She wasn't laughing.

Attempting to count the cars ahead of them, she grew anxious. The line was the longest she'd ever seen, and they'd been on the ferry hundreds of times. They'd be stuck waiting for that dumb ferry for hours! To make things worse, the men who sold sno cones and candy never came to the cars at the end of the line. They always hung around the front, near the restrooms. Even if they did come to their car, Mama would try to talk Daddy out of buying anything. She always did.

Sara felt like crying as they sat in the station wagon waiting for the line to creep up. It was hot even with the windows rolled down and her feet sticking out. There was nothing to do. Nothing. They had played all the games Mama brought with them a long time ago and read all the books Mama had checked out of the Rosenberg Library.

"Daddy, can I get out and walk around?" she whined after they'd been in line for a while. "It's too hot to just sit here and wait for that stupid old ferry."

"Sure," Daddy said, turning in his seat and smiling at them. "Get out and stretch your legs. You'll feel better. All you kids get out and stretch your legs. Keep on the right side of the road so Mama can watch you though."

"I don't want to get out," her sister moaned from the other side of the middle seat. The boys were scrambling out the back window, getting cool, and Sara was stuck listening to her old sister.

"You're going to have to move so I can get by." Sara put her tongue out in her sister's face.

"Get out on your side," the older girl said before sticking her tongue out in response.

"You just want me to get into trouble," the younger girl spouted as she started in her big sister's direction. "Move over, or I'm crawling over you."

"Mama," her sister cried, dragging the word out like it was caught in her throat. "She stuck her tongue out at me."

"Did not," Sara said as she began to push and climb toward the door.

"She did too, and she's climbing on me. Mama!"

"Move out of the way," Sara said. "I have to get out. It's too hot, and I'm dying."

"Girls!" Mama said. "Quit fighting." She looked at the older girl. "Open the door and get out so your sister doesn't have to crawl over you." Then she looked at the younger one. "I don't want you to make faces at your sister anymore. We're all tired, and it's not helping matters."

After Mama turned around, Sara's sister made a face, but she opened the door and stepped out so the littler girl could get by.

"Fatso!" Sara whispered into her sister's ear as she hopped out of the wagon.

"Mama," her big sister cried again, but Sara was running. By the time she got back, Mama would forget what the old tattletale said.

Sara ran toward the front of the line of cars. At least there was a little breeze outside the station wagon. It felt good to be almost home. She could smell the saltwater as she ran. First thing she was going to do when they got to the house, *if* they ever got to the house with all those cars, was put on her bathing suit and go jump in the bayou. Golly would that feel good.

The boys were up ahead of her, running in single file on the sand at the side of the road. Her big brother was leading the way, and her little brother was trying to keep up. She ran as fast as she could to catch up with them. She was a good runner. Her teacher had told her she could be on the relay team the next year at school.

She counted the cars as she ran, thirty-five, thirty-six—there must be a million of them. Turning, she looked at the line that had formed behind their station wagon. It went on and on until it was out of sight around the sand dunes. Boy, was she glad they had gotten there when they had.

She turned back. Her brothers had come to a halt and were waiting for her, so she ran faster. Both of them frowned in her direction.

"What's the matter?" she asked, out of breath when she caught up with them.

"Sis, there's a car up ahead that's pulled out of line," her older brother said, shaking his head.

Sara's stomach practically fell out onto the sand. "Oh no!" They all knew what that meant. She glanced at her younger brother's little face. Even he knew what would happen. Daddy would spot the car and want to help. They'd *never* get home.

She looked behind them at the cars still waiting in line. The station wagon was out of sight, but as soon as the next ferry took on cars and the line moved up, Daddy would see those people at the side of the road.

"Maybe they'll get their problem fixed before Daddy sees them," she said.

"Somebody else might help," her little brother said.

"And get out of this ferry line?" her older brother asked. "Nah."

"What are we going to do?" Sara looked to her big brother for a solution.

"I don't know, but once Dad sees them, we're a goner."

"Let's run up there and see what's the matter. Maybe we can help before Daddy pulls the car up here," Sara suggested.

The three kids broke into a run again and headed toward the disabled car. As they grew closer, a man lifted the hood and stuck his head underneath. Three little boys played in the sand nearby, and a lady fanned herself with a paper bag.

"We're sunk now," Sara yelled as they ran.

"Yeah," her older brother replied, "little kids. Our Good Samaritan's a sucker for them every time."

Sara stopped, looked at her brother, and laughed. At least she knew now what they called her daddy. Taking a deep breath, she ran toward the people in the disabled car as fast as she could to see how she could help.

QUEEN FOR A DAY

A Memoir

After Hurricane Carla, my mother got a job at the Galveston Convention and Visitors Bureau to help make money to replace our house. The four of us kids were left to our own devices. Our 18-year-old cousin, who had been raised with us, had gotten married the month prior to the hurricane, and our grandmother, who had gone to Australia to live, had not yet returned.

Mama worked all day at the "tourist bureau" as we called it. She would hurry home to cook dinner and yell at us before Daddy arrived, which wasn't difficult to do since he often stayed at his law office until very late. We lived in a small three-bedroom "camp" on Offatts Bayou, down the oyster shell road from where our house had been before the tornado, spawned by Hurricane Carla, destroyed it. We were lucky there was something left standing in our neighborhood to rent.

It wasn't that Mama had never worked before; she had. After WWII, she came here from England. While Dad was finishing his education and she was having babies, she'd enrolled in a secretarial course. When Dad opened his law office in Galveston, Mama became Dad's legal secretary. But as finances improved, she'd been able to stay at home with the four of us. Five, if you counted various cousins on my father's side who lived with us from time-to-time.

By the time Hurricane Carla blew in, we were eleven, twelve, thirteen, and fourteen. In the mornings, Mom rose way before us. She would make our lunches, wake us up, holler at us until we got out of bed and dressed and ate something, and kick us out the door in time to catch the bus. She'd also run a load of laundry and hang it out on the line to dry.

We rode the school bus from one end of the island to the other. Mama saw us off at 7:15 in the morning, and we'd greet her at the door at 5:30 in the evening, or later if she had to pick one of us up from an after-school practice. She'd cook dinner, feed the animals, straighten up the house, make sure we did our homework instead of watching television, and gather in the laundry. Most of the time, she'd stay up until Dad got home from his law practice, which often was as late as midnight, and warm up a meal for them to eat together. Of course, on PTA night, Mom would go to the PTA meetings at our schools, or attend open houses, confer with our teachers, and often bake goodies for the fundraiser.

On weekends, Mom would tackle the big chores. She would launder more clothes, change the sheets, wash the windows, vacuum the floors, shop for massive amounts of groceries, pay the bills, drag us fussing and fighting to church, and try to squeeze in a nap on the afternoons. She would also run us to our extra-curricular activities if an event took place over the weekend and, of course, stay and watch.

Dad, as an attorney and a politician, always had someplace to be. If he wasn't at his law office or visiting people around town, there were fairs, craft shows, parades, fundraisers, rodeos, and dinners he had to be at to work the crowd and win votes for whatever he happened to be running for that year. Mama, her red hair shining in the sun, stood by his side, quietly in the background, smiling, nodding, supporting him every handshake of the way.

If, on the weekends, no outside events drew Dad, he would invite folks to our house to fish, swim, go for boat rides, or break bread with us. The aroma of garlic French bread wafted through our house on those Sunday afternoons as Mom put out basket after basket, together with whatever food she could rustle up out of the refrigerator or freezer and cook really quick if people showed up after our Sunday dinner. I remember Mama termed herself the chief-cook-and-bottle-washer. That apt description brings back memories even now, though all of us kids only knew her as Mama.

On weekday afternoons, when I arrived home from school, I always turned on the television and tuned to a program called "Queen for a Day." I'd listen to the ladies tell their sad stories. I'd vote with the audience, clapping my hands for the lady who deserved the honor the most. When the Queen was chosen, I'd listen intently to the vast array of prizes she'd been awarded as she brushed away her tears of joy. And all the while I'd think, *My mama could use a clothes dryer, so she doesn't have to stand out there under the porch and hang out the clothes in all that wind. We could sure use one of those automatic dishwashers in our kitchen with all the dirty dishes that show up every day. Boy, would a new steam iron be great so water wouldn't have to be sprinkled on the clothes from an RC bottle with a stopper stuck in it.* My mama needed all those things every bit as much as those ladies on the television.

I don't remember Mama ever being sick when we were growing up. I guess she didn't have time. What I remember is her always having a tissue tucked up her sleeve, frequently pulling it out, wiping her nose, and pushing it back up her sleeve again.

I saw Mama cry very few times, though I'm not sure now what caused her tears. I suspect Mama cried when she arrived in this country after the war and learned that her father had died of tuberculosis back in England while she was on a ship crossing the ocean. I suspect she probably was reduced to tears the day we drove back over the Causeway Bridge and found that a tornado had destroyed our brand-new house. I suspect she cried the day my older brother accidentally shot my younger brother, and again when she learned that my brother would live. And she must have cried the four times my father almost died too young but was pulled through by the miracles of modern science. I suspect she cried the day her mother died. I know she cried when she learned her only brother, who she had seen one time in fifty years, had left this world, and she would never get a chance to tell him goodbye.

What I do know is the day I cried for her. The day twenty-three years after my parents' beautiful dream home was smashed by a tornado. I happened to drop by their house and find Mama sitting at the dining table, bills spread around her, writing out checks. She looked up from her chore and said to me, with a small smile on her face and a check she'd made out in her hand, "I just paid the last installment on the house we lost in Hurricane Carla."

I realized then that my quiet mama, while never appearing on television, while never being applauded by an audience of hundreds of people, while never being crowned with rhinestones and cloaked in a fake fur cape, and while deserving of the honor of "Queen for a Day" didn't need those superficial things. My mama, Jean Margaret Attwood Baker, with her big heart and quiet ways, who never complained, who worked tirelessly inside the home and out, who endured hardships after the war in a new country without family to turn to, didn't need to be "Queen for a Day." She was already Queen for a Lifetime.

I awoke in Okinawa, Japan in 1971 and found myself married to a soldier and mother of a two-month-old daughter. How did I get there?

MY RUDE AWAKENING

As a child of the 60s, I was radical, hard-headed, immature, confused, and, I guess you could say, a hell-raiser. During my second year of college, my parents asked me to drop-out rather than waste any more of their hard-earned money. So I did, reluctantly. I had no idea what I would do, but then I had no plan for my life before I ever entered college. With great apprehension, I contacted a friend who lived in the Washington D.C. area and asked to stay with her until I found a job and a place to live. The night I arrived, I met my future husband.

Not having any real skills, I don't know how I thought I would support myself. But that goes with the immature part. I didn't know any better, didn't realize I could do nothing really marketable except type. In college, I'd enrolled in typing and shorthand in case I needed to get a job. I typed twenty-two words a minute when the Riggs National Bank personnel department tested me. Laughable as that was, someone must have taken pity on me. They hired me to work in the steno-pool.

Grateful and elated, I began living as an independent young woman on my $4200 annual salary. The year was 1969, and I was nineteen. War raged in Viet Nam. People marched on the capitol. And the army drafted my boyfriend.

When he returned from basic training, my boyfriend and I were married. We lived together until he received orders for Nam. Then, sad on many levels, we drove home to my parents' where he left me and flew to the other side of the world.

I apparently became pregnant on the eve of my husband's departure. Though I obtained a job at an insurance company, they fired me when I informed them of my status, the boss saying I should be home with my feet up. Disgusted, but knowing I'd have the same problem everywhere I applied, I gave up my job search. For nine months, I spent my time writing letters, playing solitaire, watching TV, and sleeping. After I gave birth to our daughter, caring for my baby added to my list of activities.

My parents did everything. I slept in my old bedroom, ate their food, and used my army allotment check for the car payment, credit card bill, and maternity clothes. My mother cooked, cleaned, laundered, and generally ran the household. I behaved like a child—a child having a child—and didn't realize how easy I had it.

When my husband returned from Viet Nam, we drove across the country both ways and visited relatives for two weeks. Our journey ended in California where we boarded a plane for a twenty-hour flight to Okinawa, Japan. Okinawa, one of the rocky Ryukyu Islands, the scene of horrific, bloody fighting during World War II, had been U.S. occupied ever since.

We rented an unfurnished, little stone house off base about a mile from the gate. Like in a wilderness, the grass surrounding the place was taller than we were, which concerned us because of habu snakes* whose bite, we'd heard, would be an immediate

* Habus are pit vipers (or called tree vipers)

death sentence. During the time we lived there, we found a habu on a tree outside our bedroom window.

Okinawa is also a habitat for odd-looking, slimy, pale green lizards with suction cup feet. They'd scurry upside down through the gaps between the walls and roof of our house. They croaked not unlike frogs, their gullets bouncing up and down as though a tiny ball rebounded inside when they made that peculiar noise. I got the willies when I'd enter or exit the house and one would fall in my hair.

The humidity—well, to put it mildly, the moist breezes of the Texas Gulf Coast where I'd grown up had nothing on the Ryukyu Islands. I'd scarcely step outside the door before feeling like I'd been mugged by warm, soggy air.

Here is the definition of a rude awakening: a twenty-one-year-old girl opening her eyes one morning and finding herself in a country in which English is the second language, married to a soldier she hadn't even known a couple of years earlier, mother of a two-month-old daughter—albeit a gorgeous, well-behaved baby—and broker than Cooter Brown was drunk. Bewildered, I wondered how in the hell I got there.

Not only did my mom live thousands of miles away, so I had no one to lean on, ask questions of, or learn from, but so did my husband's mother. Not only were we strangers in a foreign land, but we were distanced from other Americans because we lived off base and knew nary a soul. Long-distance phone calls cost a fortune back then. And letters and parcels traveled on the proverbial "slow boat."

The first few months of the fourteen we lived there held a steep learning curve. Finding American-sized furniture proved to be impossible. I'm not exactly an Amazon at five-feet-eight inches, but I felt like one when I sat down on Japanese chairs and my knees seemed to be as high as my chin. We made do though, decorating with brown cardboard appliance boxes, sewing curtains from cheap fabric we found in the market after my sewing machine arrived, using make-shift cookware such as a cookie sheet on which to broil chicken, and learning how a family of three could live on a Specialist Five's meager salary.

Raising our baby was as trial and error as it would have been at home, except we had few luxuries. We did, however, have an abundance of love and sprinkled that liberally around her. She flourished like a forsythia plant bursting into bloom. And the under-funded base library, which we were fortunate even to have, provided helpful books, such as one on how to teach your baby to read.

Learning to be a proper enlisted-man's wife was one of "If at first you don't succeed…." I often remembered what the Lutheran minister said during the counseling classes prior to our wedding. My obligation as a wife was to get my husband out of bed every morning, feed him a nourishing breakfast, and launch him off to work on time.

I'm afraid in my quest to be that person, that loving wife and mother, I took my "duties" too much to heart. Another Army wife told me a story about a woman who would get up every morning, cook breakfast for her husband and son, and send them off to work always with a kiss goodbye in case something happened while they were gone. There came a day, however, when the dutiful wife and mother decided she had tired of that laborious routine, so she didn't get up with them. They were killed on the way to work.

Well, if I'd been lead-bottomed before hearing that, I would change my ways, even though soldiers had to arise and set off for the base before the sun's rays began peering over the horizon. The next morning, I dragged myself out of bed in the dead of dark, splashed my face with water, and entered our little kitchen to make my husband the perfect breakfast. I boiled the water, poached two eggs, toasted and buttered two slices of bread, poured orange juice, and set the table beautifully with knife, fork, and spoon in place and napkin neatly folded.

I can still see myself tiptoeing into the bedroom, turning on the lamp, and nudging him awake.

"Time to get up. Your breakfast is ready," I said, proud to have laid out such a spread.

He grumbled and groaned and said, "Honey, can't you see it's still the middle of the night?" And turned away from where I stood.

The bedside clock read 2:30 a.m. With my 20-20 vision, how had I mistaken the time when I crawled out of bed? In my head I asked, "Can't you get up and eat it anyway since I went to all this trouble?"

Exasperated with myself, I turned out the light and fell back into bed. When I arose with the baby's cries a number of hours later, my husband had reported for duty. The breakfast still sat where I'd left it, perfectly poached eggs with golden yokes like huge pupils, on perfectly toasted bread, in a perfect place setting on our little, wobbly dinette table.

Chuckling at myself, I realized that though I was all grown up, I didn't have to take everything so seriously, not to mention literally. I was married with a baby, an adult with responsibilities. Everything did not have to be perfect for life to work out for this new wife and mother.

This is an autobiographical piece I wrote after my first divorce. I confess I thought about editing out some of the more embarrassing confessions, but the statute of limitations has long run on my offenses, and the other embarrassing bits I can live with.

THE DARK CHILD

Was it my destiny to end up in the state court system or would my life have been different if my mother, father, or grandmother had paid more attention to me? I pondered those questions recently, when I found a fifty-year-old photograph of my English grandmother with the four of us little kids. On my grandmother's right stands my towheaded big sister, on her left, my towheaded big brother. My towheaded baby brother, wearing nothing but a diaper, sits in her arms. I stand in front of my grandmother, in the shadows, the dark child.

My grandmother always favored my little brother. I remember when she arrived from England and took over one of the rooms in our small house. Mama and Daddy had a room to themselves. The four of us slept in one room in bunk beds. Granny got the other one. I have no idea what her room looked like. She wouldn't let any of us inside, except him, my little brother. He and I would go to the door and knock. Granny would open the door, scoop him up, and shut the door in my face. Sometimes she would give me a lemon drop first. Until her death at ninety, she always kept a tin of lemon drops nearby.

I am not surprised that in the photograph my grandmother is holding my baby brother with both hands. I only wonder why she didn't ever hold me. Perhaps because I wasn't the littlest. I was the littlest girl, though. And I was the only brown-headed child in that family of blondes. My mother had red hair. My father had black. My sister and brothers used to tell me I was adopted, but I always replied, "I'm the only one who looks like Daddy. The milkman must have brought you." It was my only defense.

When I figured out as I grew older that I really was the only one who looked like our father, I used that to my advantage because, after all, I didn't feel special in that family. I wasn't a boy. I wasn't the oldest. I wasn't even the oldest girl. I was the second middle child. While my sister was eighteen months older, my little brother was inconsiderate enough to be only thirteen months younger. I really didn't get enough time with our mother. And on top of that, my grandmother moved in.

I understand now, as an adult, that life was hectic for Mama, a young English war bride in a strange land, whose employment included collecting the money from washers and dryers in washeterias all over Houston. But at the time, Mama's difficulties didn't matter. I was a child and the world revolved around me. I remember that, day and night, my mama drove around Houston in her little Studebaker with two children in the front seat and two in the back. At least I got to sit in the front with my little brother, though he got to sit next to Mama.

Children may not understand what is going on, but we do remember things. I remember Mama talking to us as she drove. One time, Mama said she was lost, that she had driven over the same road more than once. I remember an incident that sounds like it's fiction but is not. It was a dark and rainy night. Mama pulled over to the side of the road. She lectured the four of us to be good, that she'd be right back. She stepped out into the rain and found the cat she'd run over. Taking it into her arms and cuddling it, Mama walked from door-to-door, knocking and asking for its owners.

If children are very young, they don't know why they do certain things. That's why we have laws that don't hold children responsible until they are around ten years old, arguably the age of reason. And thank goodness for that or I, for one, would have a rap sheet the length of a yard stick. Children sometimes have an irresistible impulse to behave in unacceptable ways, such as throwing temper tantrums, hitting others, biting, taking what isn't theirs, and running away from home. They behave in ways that would tell an observer a problem child is developing, though the parents might not notice for a while. The parents may be too busy. Or in denial about their child's behavior problems, much like an alcoholic might be in denial about his drinking problems.

My father was a tall, lanky storyteller, who, when he laughed, would put his head back and let go with guffaws that filled observers with such glee that tears would often spill from their eyes. Trouble was, I didn't see my father much when I was little. I was too young at three years of age to comprehend why he was gone or, if he was at home, why he was shut behind a door with his face buried in a book, telling me to go away when I would open the door a crack and peek at him. I didn't know he was trying to get a college education and it wouldn't have mattered if I had. I still would have suffered the loss of him.

As it turned out, the lack of attention I was given caused me to turn to a life of crime. The root of the evil that possessed me was chocolate ice cream. Mama wouldn't buy me chocolate ice cream whenever I wanted it, but if Daddy was around, I could pull on his hand, look up at the sky where his face was, ask him in my best voice, and presto, an ice cream would magically appear in my hand. Well, as I said, he was awfully busy with those books at night and gone so much the rest of the time.

One day, I took my little brother by the hand. He must have been at least two by then, which would have made me three. I walked him all the way down to the end of the block to the grocery store on the corner. When we found the long horizontal cabinet that held the ice cream, I slid open the glass door, stood on my tip toes, leaned over, put the top half of my body inside, and searched until I found the chocolate cups. I must have looked like a swimmer breast stroking out of water as I reached in with both hands and teetered on my midriff. I remember my body rocking and thought I would dive in before I finally managed to drop back down to the floor, two cups of chocolate ice cream in my possession. Pulling the paper wrapper off two spoon-shaped wooden paddles, I gave one to my brother and we consumed our treats before arriving back down the block at our house. I was well-pleased with myself until Mama confronted me at the door. I'm not sure how she knew what I had done, but she took us, one in each hand, and marched us all the way back down the street. Tears rolled down my cheeks as she made us each give a nickel to the old man behind the counter and apologize for stealing his ice cream. It was the first time I knew I had done something really wrong. The old man tried to refuse the nickels, but, of course, my mother wouldn't accept no.

Was it my criminal inclinations that made me feel as though I must have been born to the wrong family? Or was it the feeling I must have been born to the wrong family that fueled my criminal inclinations? I can only wonder, but I never felt as though I belonged in that family of blondes. I often felt angry and can remember assaulting my siblings on more than one occasion. I once broke a hairbrush over my sister's head. I stabbed my little brother in the forehead with a pencil. And one time, I stabbed my big brother in the thigh with a pencil for tickling me when I was trying to hold my breath as we drove all the way across the causeway bridge on the way home after church.

Mama was so tight with money that, as they say, she still had half the first penny she'd ever received. When we four children turned six, we each received a quarter allowance. On every birthday, she gave us a nickel raise.

Yes, I could earn extra money. Being only in elementary school, I was far too young to get a job outside of the house, but Mama would pay for extra chores. I could iron Daddy's shirts for ten cents apiece. Three handkerchiefs for a nickel. And I can remember even earlier than that, when Mama paid us to catch flies.

You heard me. We received a penny for every five flies. And they'd better be dead. Furthermore, she had better not catch us holding the screen door open to let in any more flies. Back then, we lived on Offatts Bayou and had chickens, some geese, always at least one cat and dog, and the fish and crabs we'd catch and bring into the kitchen. There were lots of flies.

Life at my school was hard and confusing. A couple of new neighborhoods had been built. New kids had moved in. Now, not only did I feel that I didn't belong in my birth family, but I didn't fit in at school. All the new, rich kids took over. They became the most popular. They became student council representatives and by the sixth grade, the officers. They always had nice clothes and money to spend. My mother had continued with my nickel raises. By sixth grade I made fifty cents a week for washing the dishes three times a week, making my half of the bed I shared with my sister, and keeping my half of our room clean. Frugal with everything, Mama also doled out the notebook paper ten sheets at a time. And since milk at school cost four cents, she gave us a nickel on Monday, Tuesday, Wednesday, and Thursday. Each day we had to return the change to her. On Friday, she would give us the four pennies change to buy our milk. You can see how it was, can't you?

Things did not improve as the years went by. No other family ever came forward to claim me. I learned to confess my guilt, because I always got caught anyway. Finally, I quit committing those crimes. But an interesting twist came about. I started being blamed for everything bad that happened at our house.

Once, my older brother cut his foot on barnacles on our pier and ran into the house, poured alcohol over his foot, dried it off with the towel hanging on the rack in our parents' bathroom, put the towel back, and didn't tell anyone. When my mother washed her face and dried it in the towel of alcohol, she was so angry she rushed into the dining room where we kids were sitting around the table and rubbed the towel in my face. My brother had the good grace to admit he was the offender, not me, but I never received an apology.

Another time, after my brother and sister started smoking cigarettes behind our parents' back, one of them burned a hole in the coffee table. My mother accused me of the crime and would not believe my protestations of innocence.

Confusion reigned inside of me. I didn't fit into the family. I didn't fit in at school. We went to a very small church so there were no children there to be my friends. I had changed my ways but still was falsely accused of crimes. Would I ever find my niche in the world?

I was a child of the sixties. I went off to college without giving it much thought, soon hating the school in which I enrolled for my freshman year. Didn't know what to major in. Pretended to be someone I wasn't so I could fit in. I was elected to an office but was removed from that office when my grades dropped. I witnessed a near riot on our campus when Martin Luther King was murdered. Experienced sex for the first time. Lived through the death of my best friend from seventh grade. And transferred to another school. The second year I tried drugs. Some friends got hooked on heroin. My boyfriend was in love with someone else. A good friend got busted and received an unjust sentence. And my parents, who had caught on to my lifestyle, made me drop out.

With my tax refund from my job of the previous summer, I moved to the suburbs of Washington, D.C. where my older brother's fiancée lived, and began an unavowed life of poverty. I could type twenty words a minute and was hired to work in the steno pool of a huge bank. My salary was $4200 a year. Since my bit of savings ran out quickly, I was so happy to get a job that it never occurred to me to try to find one that paid better. At nineteen, I was not an assertive woman, in spite of being a product of the sixties. I had no car, no money, and no friends or relatives except for my brother's fiancée who, I discovered after I arrived, had broken up with my brother. It was only because her mother and father had been friends with my parents in 1950s Houston that I had a roof over my head. And as soon as I was paid, my brother's ex-girl and I rented an apartment.

I rode the bus to and from work and walked many blocks to get to and from the bus stop. I worked on the ninth floor of the 9th and F Branch of our bank. I wanted to lose weight, so I climbed the stairs every day when I got to work. One day as I walked to work, some construction workers whistled at me and for once I felt pretty good about myself.

I made a friend in the first few months I worked at the bank. We used to eat lunch together. Her name was Geneva, and she had a great smile. Sometimes, if we had any money left in our paychecks, we would go shopping at the large department store that was near the bank. I thought our friendship was progressing nicely and felt I finally had found where I fit in when, all of a sudden, she was transferred to another branch of the bank. I knew I would never see Geneva again, because I lived in one suburb of D.C. and she, in another, and neither of us had any transportation. Neither did we understand why they sent her away so unexpectedly. Later,

I was told it was because Geneva was black and I, white. I didn't see a future in banking after that.

Money was more than a bit tight. My share of the rent was ninety-five dollars a month. I paid forty-five cents each way for the bus. I learned to economize. I bought three pot pies for a dollar. I would have no breakfast, a hotdog and a coke for lunch, and a pot pie for dinner. It wasn't long before I caught the flu for the first time in my life and acquired doctor bills.

Before my brother's ex-fiancée and I parted ways, she fixed me up with a young man who I had met the first night I was in northern Virginia. When I got the flu, he came over and took care of me. Shortly thereafter, I moved in with him and his sister. For the first time in my life, not only did we have cockroaches crawling on the kitchen counters in the middle of the night when you turned on the light but crawling on the walls all around the apartment in broad daylight. I learned to live with them. And they with me.

Viet Nam was in full force. On weekends, protesters lined the streets. My relationship with Peter grew more serious as we went on motorcycle rides, picnics, bicycling, and began sleeping together. After he was drafted, he called me from basic training and proposed. I accepted. We were married as soon as he completed his training. In the meantime, I scraped up the money to go down to Ft. Benning, Georgia to see him on the first weekend he was free. After he returned to the base, I was walking to the bus for a ride to the airport when some boys drove by and called me a whore. So much for free love and my self-esteem.

After my husband got orders for Viet Nam, I went home. The year I was there, I was unable to get a job because I was pregnant. I lived with my parents. One high school friend was married and had a baby, but everyone else was away at college. The year after that, the baby and I went to Okinawa, Japan with my husband. For the first time in my life I knew what it was like to be a minority. While we were there, our country gave Okinawa back to the

Japanese. I awoke one morning to the "Rising Sun" flying from a flagpole. I had been more than ready to go home before that, but I was stuck until we could all go home together.

I was bored. We were broke. When the locals went on strike, I found work for two weeks unloading crates of clothing in the warehouse of the PX. It was the only job an army wife could get. Shortly after that, there was a shipping strike on the west coast. For months, we couldn't even get a box of Kraft Macaroni and Cheese. I remember the day we arrived back in California and picked up our car. My husband pulled into a grocery store parking lot and stayed with the baby while I went inside to purchase bread, lunchmeat, and fruit for our picnic lunch. The next thing I knew, he was shaking my arm and calling my name. I found myself in the produce section of the grocery store, my eyes fixed on the vast array of fresh fruits and vegetables.

During the fourteen months we lived in Okinawa, I tried several times to fit in with the other wives. We lived off base so, as a rule, the people who lived on base didn't associate with us. One day, I was getting my hair done when the woman in the salon chair next to me struck up a conversation. As she got up to leave, she remarked that she would like me to join the wives club. For the first time since I arrived, I felt a surge of hope. I replied that I would love to be a member, my heart soaring at the invitation. Just before she departed, though, she asked me what rank my husband was. When she heard that he was not an officer, she apologized and said that the club was for officers' wives only.

During those months, I decided I wanted an education. I sent for college catalogs. My husband told me I could go if I could figure out what to do with the baby and if I could find the money. So I did. And I decided I wanted to be a probation officer.

When we moved back to the states, we moved to Arlington, Texas. For two years, I worked on my bachelor's degree. Later, we moved to Galveston, where I was from. My husband broke his foot right before we moved and anything we had saved was spent before his foot healed and he could get a job. I still hadn't graduated, but we needed money, so I went back to work at a bank. When I asked one of the officers what my future would be at the bank, he said that if he had a choice between promoting a female or a black person (only he didn't use the word black), he guessed he would have to promote the female. Again, I decided banking wasn't for me.

It wasn't long before I became pregnant again. And about that time, I heard about a new university that had opened up about forty-five minutes from our apartment. I made my plans once again and worked overtime at the bank, paying off bills so I could go back to school, this time to finish my degree. I also borrowed some money. At six months pregnant, I quit my job and enrolled in the upper level university. A few months later, I gave birth to a second daughter. Ten days after that, I was back in school. The following year, I finally was awarded my bachelor's degree in criminal justice. It only took nine and one-half years.

I worked at various jobs and kept applying for a position as a probation officer. Two years later, I landed the coveted job. In the meantime, I decided I wanted to go to law school. I applied and got accepted at the same time I landed the probation job. I began to do both at the same time. I didn't have time to develop close relationships at the office or at law school, because I had spread myself too thin. For three years, I worked and commuted fifty miles to school each way and studied every spare minute while trying to find time for my husband and children.

When I became a lawyer, I was thirty-two years old, much older than all the other "baby" lawyers. I shared office space with two much older male lawyers who had been law partners with my father (after a brief stint with two female lawyers, which didn't work out). Eight years later, I was the first woman in our county to run for judge. My presence came as a shock to the much older male judges, who didn't think I could win. They adjusted, of course, but things were never the same for them, and certainly there was never a sense of belonging for me. It had become a way of life for me, by then, the feeling that I never fit in. I had learned to live with it. On the outside, I gave no sign it was of any consequence and went about being the first proactive judge in our county.

A number of years ago, after my divorce, I visited England. I had gone to a conference but had scheduled a week's vacation afterward. During that time, I had the opportunity to go into the countryside to visit my grandmother's eighty-four-year-old cousin, Raymond. This was long after Granny's death. I had planned an excursion, but because he spoke English and I spoke American, we missed each other. I had taken a train, but he had told me to take a bus. By the time I figured out that I had misunderstood him, I had gone to the bus station looking for him and, I found out later, he had gone to the train station looking for me. Finally at the end of the day, I returned to my room, resigned that I would not get to visit my cousin in spite of a great desire in my heart to do so. I mourned that missed opportunity as though Raymond had died, for at his advanced age, I knew I might not ever get to see him.

My roommate and I planned several other tours, but none of them brought me joy. Finally, our last day came around. We had special plans for an evening excursion when I decided nothing was as important to me as seeing my cousin. I phoned his house, and his ailing wife answered. She said he would be delighted, that he had been broken-hearted at our near miss. I hopped a train for his village. This time it worked to perfection. As soon as I saw the white-haired old cherub, I had an immediate and unexplained affinity for him, as though we'd known each other before. It was, for me, love at first sight. When he took me for a tour of his village, where many of my ancestors had lived, my mother's mother's people, and when he took me to the church the family had attended, and we walked into the graveyard to see his first wife's grave, and when he showed me the view from the bluff, and our ancestors' paintings hanging on his walls, I finally felt I'd found where I belonged. My childhood experiences no longer mattered. My lifelong desire to find where I fit dissolved. It was not important that the feeling might not last. It was enough for me that in a few short hours the blanks in my life had been filled in. It didn't matter that I was the dark child anymore.

This is a piece I wrote not very long after my second husband and I moved to Fredericksburg, Texas, after I retired from the bench.

I DIDN'T BURN THE HOUSE DOWN

For Christmas one year, Mama gave us all $100 gift cards. I went right out to Sam's where, for $34.84, I found Microsoft Office 2003, 11 Program Tutorial Set. Oh boy, I would be able to update my computer software to the 2003 version of everything. This was really important to me since I was getting ready to launch a marketing plan for my books and start a seminar business. It did seem awfully cheap, but I figured they were getting ready to come out with the 2004 version ergo, unloading the 2003. Fine, I'd worry about 2004 in 2005 or 2006. I was staying in the present moment.

When I arrived home, I dumped the bag out and prepared to begin. A number of years ago, I bought scissors that could cut through anything, including a penny. The salesman demonstrated for me. I'm not sure why you would want to cut a penny, but I remember taking them from him, examining them, and immediately cutting a hole in the knee of my pants. I've kept those scissors all these years. I was awarded them in the divorce.

Faced with the hard, plastic-encased box of Microsoft software, Office 2003 Edition, I knew that my special scissors were the answer to actually getting into the box, much less the plastic cases inside that held each little CD. After about seven minutes of chopping, I rescued the cardboard box from the plastic encasement. Inside said cardboard box were five CDs. I immediately opened the first one, pressed the tiny button on my computer where the tray comes out, and dropped in the CD. Various and sundry words popped onto the screen and instructed me to find the CD for some software I didn't own.

I'm neither admitting nor denying I have a college degree, much less a law degree. I can not only read, but I can write the English language. You've heard of legalese? What I don't seem to comprehend is computerese. When I picked up the box I saw in bold, white on royal blue letters **LEARN2**. LEARN THE FAST AND EASY WAY.

Okay. It was only $34.84, and I didn't pay for it anyway, my mother did. But I'd convinced myself if I wanted to have an effective marketing plan, I needed new, up-to-date software. I lived in a small town and didn't want to drive thirty minutes to an office supply store, so I logged onto Amazon, which has Microsoft software in stock. Just what I needed, Microsoft Office 2003 Professional Upgrade. I read the system requirements. Microsoft Windows 2000 with Service Pack 3, MICROSOFT Windows XP, or a later operating system. I had Windows ME. Millennium means 2000, ergo I had Windows 2000. That was the product for me. Excited, I pushed all the right buttons and charged the upgrade to my American Express, only $279.99 plus tax, title, and license. I went back to working on my novel. By the next week when it arrived, I would have another chapter done and not feel guilty taking from my writing time to install and learn my new, updated, office management system.

Eventually, I looked outside the door one day and there sat a box from Amazon with my name on it. I hurriedly cut it and the plastic coffin with my trusty, ever-sharp scissors and found my Microsoft Office Professional Edition 2003, Upgrade. That box truly included everything I would ever need to run my writing and seminar business from my home. Was I clever or what?

I shut down every program and proceeded to install the wonder products, not stopping to clap my hands with glee. I popped in the first CD when the little drawer thing came out of my computer and immediately received an error message. My computer couldn't find my edition of Windows 2000 or XP. I knew I had 2000. I remember when I bought the computer, it came already installed. I figured out how to find what version I had, clicking on one thing and another until I found the right button. Windows ME. Same thing, isn't it? It's got to be. ME means 2000. I put the CD in and out of the tray thingy several times but always got the same message. Well, not to worry, I'd go to the Help place and ask them how to get it to work with ME. After about thirty minutes of clicking on stuff at the online Help place and not finding how to actually email a question to anyone, be it Microsoft people or any computer nerd sitting out there in the community and waiting for questions to come in from novices (and I say that generously for my own ego) like me, I decide to do what only a rational, sane, college-educated person would do. I drove to Walmart. Walmart, thank the higher power, had a box that said Microsoft Windows XP Home Edition. $99.00 plus the usual add-ons.

This time, I asked the woman at the counter what could I do if this was not the correct product and my other, wonderful, new, up-to-date software wouldn't coordinate with this Home Edition. "Bring it back and tell the returns people I said it was okay," she said. Fine.

While I was there, I bought a combination CD, Cassette, AM/FM player for my office. Regularly $39.95, on sale after Christmas for $25.00. I'd had a discussion with my husband recently when I wanted to order a similar thing from Amazon. He'd discouraged me, telling me that it was junk, and we'd get a good one later. But he was out of town. And I was standing right in front of this one. And I could play three CDs without reloading.

Back at home with my new software and my new music box, I got out my scissors and cut the plastic theft discourager from the cardboard box, pulled out the CD, and began the install. A sign of relief escaped my lips until I saw an error message that said I needed to clean the disk. I cleaned it with a nice, soft cloth I kept beside my chair in a drawer. There did seem to be a little smudgy stuff on the shiny underside. I put it back in. It popped out, same error message. That went on three times until I saw in fine print something about that being the Office Professional Edition. The stupid computer thought I still had the other disk in that drive. Easy to fix. Shut down, restart. Even I could do that. I did that. Put in the disk. It worked. A drum roll went off in my head.

While it was installing, I pulled out my new CD/cassette/radio, using my trusty scissors to cut what now appeared to be additional layers of plastic tape over the original factory ones. Someone had purchased and returned that box. Well, at least I knew it worked if Walmart put it back in the box and sealed it up and put it back on the shelf. Pushing aside writers' books and magazines on a shelf, I assembled my new music maker and plugged it in. I saw a hole in the plastic bag that held the remote, but the remote, to my relief, was still there. I inserted three CDs, turned it on, and Mozart blasted me into the next block. It worked. Relief. I adjusted the volume with the big knob. Lower. Lower—not lower. The volume was stuck at an impossible level. Perhaps I could disable one speaker. Wait, only one speaker was working. I had to admit, my husband was right. For $25.00 what you get is cheesy. Luckily, he was not home.

As I packed up my music maker, I looked over my shoulder and saw an error message on my computer, which had been installing all that time. *Disable virus software.* Oh, poop. I clicked on the error message, but the machine was all locked up. Out came my trusty, no, not scissors, but bent paperclip and I, with some trepidation, punched the tiny little hole that contained a reset button.

After my nap, when I awakened remembering I didn't save the last chapter of my novel on a disk or the last version of an essay I'd been working on for months, and wondering if my paperclip had caused the computer to crash, I jumped out of bed and ran into my office to see whether my computer would start up. It did. First thing I did was backup those documents. Then I printed hard copies to be sure. Then I got out my Norton book and researched how to uninstall.

While that was going on, I continued packing up my music box to take out to the garage to return to the store. But first, I remembered I had to have a late Christmas gift for a friend. I'd intended to make her a candle in a china teacup glued to a matching saucer. I had even set out the wax, wick, and scent and pulled out the little pan in which to melt it. I would start melting the wax while I put the music box into the car. So I set the flame on low, put the wax and scent into the pan, and went back into my office to finish packing up the music maker into its box, trying three times to get the little wire thingy around the wadded-up cord. I finally got it into the car when I remembered I had left the three CDs inside. Unpacking, I had to find a plug in the garage to get the changer to move around so I could take out my CDs, which I did, then gave up on getting the little wire thingy around the cord again and stuffed the thing back in the box and into the back seat of the car. When I went back inside the house, I remembered the CDs on top of the trash can and returned outside for them.

Back in my office, I found Norton was uninstalled, so I pulled that disk out and inserted the Microsoft software. I was home free at last.

But wait, what was that smell? Strong. Lilacs. Moments later in the kitchen, I peered through the thick smoke, relieved there was not a fire on my stove, just thick, rising, fumy smoke from the burning wax. I turned off the burner.

Returning to my office, I saw the software was completing its installation.

I headed back to the kitchen, where I flipped on the fan over the stove and opened two windows just as my husband arrived home. When he opened the door and wrinkled his nose, I said, "Well, at least I didn't burn the house down."

Fiction

This foundation for this story was a young couple, clients of mine when I was practicing law, who fled from his mother to Louisiana and returned after the baby grew sick and died. They buried the baby somewhere in Louisiana.

NINA

Sophie waited until Frank rolled out of bed and left for work before she packed up. She mixed the baby's formula and filled the bottles. She loaded a grocery bag with her clothes. The diaper bag, she stuffed with Nina's clothes, the last of the plastic diapers, and the still-warm bottles. After double-wrapping Nina in baby blankets, Sophie hurried to her SUV before Frank, as he often did, found some reason to return.

He was checking on her. She knew that's what he was doing, as if he were waiting to catch her doing something she shouldn't.

Over the last few months, Sophie'd been able to hold back a little of the grocery money occasionally, saving a hundred dollars and change. She'd wanted it to be more, but just couldn't wait. After he'd punched her again the night before, she knew it had to be now. A hollow feeling in the pit of her stomach grew every time Frank threatened her. She was afraid if she didn't get out now, Frank might really hurt her, or worse, Nina. Sophie could never let him hurt her baby.

Their relationship had soured since Nina had come. Money was tighter, that was for sure, and Frank was drinking more. He was so unreasonable. If only he'd let her work. But every time she mentioned it, they got into a fight. And sometimes he'd hit her real hard. She wasn't used to that. Her grandparents hadn't raised her that way. If only they were still alive so she could go home.

Sophie had been scared to think one day Frank might turn on Nina. Or take Nina away from her like he said he would if Sophie tried to divorce him. Leaving this way, she could take Nina far away and make a home for her, just the two of them. Sophie would never let anyone hurt her baby.

Sophie drove their old SUV south. She knew of a place off the highway where they could spend the first night. In the meantime, Nina had enough formula to make it to the next morning. Sofie had made sandwiches for herself. She'd filled up with gas the day before and left the credit card on the kitchen table for Frank. She didn't want Frank to be able to trace her through her charges.

Sophie switched on the radio and sang along with the country music. The baby grinned a toothless grin. Her wispy brown hair glistened in the winter sun as it shined through the windshield.

When darkness began to surround them, they were just a few miles from the roadside park for which Sophie had aimed. Traffic had been light, so they'd made good time.

"We're here," Sophie said a few minutes later as she pulled to the side of the road.

Nina followed Sophie with her eyes and made little cooing noises. She'd been a model baby all day. Sophie had only had to stop the car a few times to change her. The territory over which they had driven was so flat that she'd been able to hold the bottle up to the baby's mouth with one hand and steer with the other. Sophie's main goal for the first few days was to put a lot of miles between herself and Frank.

The air had grown cooler as it got late. As long as they were driving, the inside of the car had stayed toasty warm, and there was nothing to worry about. After they stopped at the park, Sophie lowered the back seat and spread out a blanket, making a bed for them. She ate her last sandwich and fed the baby.

Taking Nina into the public restroom, Sophie gave her a sponge bath and put a clean nightie on her. She sat Nina in her carrier on the floor while she sponged herself off, then, shivering, hustled back to the rear of the car, where they would bed down for the night. They played together for a little while. When Nina started getting cranky, Sophie wrapped her in the blankets and settled her down. Digging around in the grocery bag, Sophie found another pair of socks, jeans, and a sweater to put on, then unfolded another blanket and pulled it over them.

The next morning, when Sophie awoke, she was chilled to the bone. A cold front had blown in during the night. Snow flurries filled the air. Inside the car, the temperature felt like twenty degrees.

Leaving Nina sleeping, Sophie climbed into the front seat, started the engine, and pushed the lever for the heater all the way to the right. As the car warmed up, Sophie drove to a gas station to fill up for the day. She was going to keep going south until she ran out of money, then she would get a job and a place for them to live.

When she came out from taking care of her personal needs, Sophie found that the baby had awakened and was lying on her little pallet playing and gurgling. Her nose was runny, and her eyes were tinged with red. Sophie fed Nina the last bottle, which she had warmed under the hot water faucet in the bathroom. She changed her and fixed her up in the front seat like the day before.

On the way out of the little town, Sophie stopped at the grocery store and purchased a loaf of bread, a slab of bologna, and some ready-made baby formula. After that, they were on their way again. She still had sixty-eight dollars and thirty-two cents. She stroked the baby's arm, proud they were managing so well.

The second day passed much like the first. Sophie only stopped periodically for restroom and lunch breaks and to change the baby. She stuck to roadside parks, so if Frank came after her, there would be no one to report seeing them. Later that afternoon, Nina's breathing became a little raspy. Her runny nose had turned stuffy and then runny again. Nina was cheerful and played at lunch, so Sophie didn't think too much about it other than to keep the heater on high to make sure the baby was warm enough.

Sophie and the cold front seemed to be traveling the same direction and the same speed. She couldn't shake it or outrun it. The second night was colder than the first. The station wagon cooled down much faster. Sophie hugged Nina to her chest to keep her warm. She didn't dare let the motor run so the heater could warm them, gasoline cost too much. During the night, Nina cried for a while for no apparent reason. Sophie knew she was keeping her warm enough. Nina wasn't wet or soiled and wouldn't take a bottle. Sophie talked to her and played with her until Nina finally went back to sleep.

As she lay curled up with the baby, Sophie began to think of Frank. Was he lonely without her? Who would take care of him? Who would cook for him and make sure he got off to work on time? Did he miss her and Nina? Was he sorry for what he'd said and done? She had to remind herself of how he'd treated her and stop feeling sorry for him.

The third day, Sophie decided to aim for Florida where the weather would be much warmer. She could get a job waiting tables in one of those big hotels in the city. She gassed up the car and bought some groceries and formula and even splurged and bought herself a soda. Until then, she'd made do with water and sandwiches. Frank would never think to look for her in Florida.

"Want to go to the beach, Nina?" Sophie smiled at Nina as she took the turnoff that led to Miami.

Nina developed a croupy cough that day. She must have caught a cold. Sophie stopped at a drugstore in one of the towns they passed through and bought some children's cold medicine and aspirin and calculated how much to give a three-month-old. She hoped she figured it out right. If Frank were there, he'd know. He always knew about things like that. It was a good thing they were only a few miles from Miami, because she only had a few dollars left.

That evening, when they reached the city, Sophie parked on a side street, bundled up Nina really well, and locked her in the car before leaving to hunt for a job. She knew no one would hire her if she came looking for a job with a baby on her hip.

Sophie walked up and down the main drag, but no one was looking for any help. Close to ten she went back to the car. Nina was coughing and her skin was warm to the touch. Sophie gave her some more medicine, fed her, and drove them back out of town to a roadside park where she lay down with the baby.

Nina was cuddly in her arms. She was such a sweet little thing, always smiling, her eyes shining. Sophie liked the way her little cheeks stayed pink, like a cherub. As she lay there, she thought of the day Frank had brought them home from the hospital. He was so proud. If only he hadn't ruined it by going out and getting drunk. She hadn't known it would get much worse.

She had heard of men who really hurt their wives. She'd seen a TV movie about it once, too. Frank wasn't that bad. He'd only given her a black eye that one time, and he'd said he was sorry the following morning. He hadn't done it again, either, just like he promised. Just threats, and a little pushing around. Except for the other night when he had hit her in the stomach. And he didn't mean to do it, he said. He probably hadn't really meant it, either, when he'd said he'd take Nina away from her.

The next day, Nina seemed to be doing a little better. She'd slept well and wasn't nearly so fussy as the day before. Sophie spent their last few dollars on formula and found the Salvation Army where she got some hot soup. She asked about spending the night there, but they were full. They didn't have any work for her, either. Times were hard, they said.

After lunch, Sophie drove to a different part of the city to apply for work. Again she bundled up the baby and left her in the car, parked on a side street. She returned, unsuccessful, in the early part of the evening. She fed and changed the baby, ate a sandwich, moved the car to another location and went out again. The result was the same. When she got back to the car, Sophie decided against returning to the roadside park. They couldn't afford to burn up the gas. She and Nina could wake early. No one would know they had spent the night right on that corner.

The baby was lying there peacefully, her raspy breathing shallow. Sophie pulled on her second layer of clothing, got under the covers, and held Nina close. She sang to her until Nina fell asleep. Her thoughts went to Frank again. Was he looking for them? In the course of the night, the baby coughed once or twice, but that was all.

When Sophie awoke the next morning, Nina was very still. Sophie couldn't hear her breathing. She put her ear to the baby's lips, but only felt the coolness of them. The pink was gone from Nina's cheeks, and she wouldn't open her eyes no matter how much Sophie shook her. Sophie sat cross-legged in the back of the old SUV rocking her little bundle back and forth in her arms as tears ran down her face. Later that day, Sophie drove to a roadside park and peeled off her top layer of clothing. She went to the restroom and washed up. When she came back, she kissed Nina and bundled her up, so she'd stay warm, and left her in the ladies' room. Then Sophie started the car and found a pay phone to call Frank collect. She just wanted to go home.

I wrote this story when, as an attorney, I had a few jury trials under my belt. Pretty much it says it all.

A STATE OF TORMENT

"And lastly, ladies and gentlemen of the jury," Joseph cocked his head to one side and frowned, then shook himself, trying to get rid of the feeling of déjà vu, "I want to thank you for your attentiveness during my summation this morning and throughout the duration of the trial." He smiled and bobbed his head at them and went to his seat.

"All right, ladies and gentlemen, that concludes the attorneys' arguments," the judge said. "You will now go to the jury room, select a presiding juror, read the charge, and begin your deliberations. When you have reached a verdict, knock on the door, and the bailiff will inform me."

After the jurors filed out of the courtroom, Joseph crossed over and shook hands with his opponent. "Good job, Andy."

"You, too, Joe. Good argument. I hope they didn't buy it." Andy laughed, sounding like an ass.

"Yeah, right. I feel the same. I'm going down for coffee. Want some?"

"Sure."

Joseph asked his client, Otis, “Want some coffee?” Otis shook his head.

When Andy and Joseph returned, there was no word, so Joseph removed his suit jacket and slung it over the back of the black cushioned chair in which he'd spent the last seven working days. He dropped into it and began doodling on a legal pad. Otis Blackburn, his client, stood staring out of the window. Drizzle came down against a backdrop of gray sky. Andy paced back and forth in front of the judge's bench, his shoes scraping the tile when he pivoted. There was a knock in the distance. Joseph jumped to his feet, his attention on the doorway, as was Andy's.

The bailiff shuffled out, smiling. He shook his head. "They want coffee."

Joseph sighed.

Andy shrugged. "Should've known."

"Yeah."

"I'm going over to my office for a few minutes," Andy said in a low voice. "Be right back."

Joseph nodded. Otis, still standing by the window, was looking at him. Joseph shook his head and walked down the hall to the court reporter's office.

"Okay if I use your phone to call my office, Carl?"

"Sure, Joe. False alarm, huh?"

"Yeah." He punched the buttons. "Joanie, it's me," he said. "The jury's been out about an hour. Just sent for refreshments, so it'll be a while. What's going on?"

"Mrs. Richardson called and wanted to know if she could get a copy of her divorce decree. I have it ready for her to pick up."

"Okay. If anyone wants appointments, make them for tomorrow. We should be done by then."

"No one has called for an appointment."

"Oh. I just thought—"

"I know. Things just haven't picked up. Sorry, Joe."

"Okay. Well, call me if you need me." He hung up.

"Thanks, Carl," he said to the reporter.

"S'all right."

Back in the courtroom, Joseph resumed his doodling. Otis was studying a newspaper he'd found someplace.

Except for the rustling of the paper when Otis turned a page, there was no noise in the courtroom. Joseph's stomach churned. He reached into his suit coat pocket and found some antacids, a bit of paper trailing away from the opened roll like a tail. He popped one into his mouth and grimaced at the chalky texture. His teeth crunched on it, breaking it into bits, the sound of it so loud in his ears that he was sure the noise echoed throughout the room. The fruity flavor replaced the aftertaste of the coffee. He replaced the roll and stared at the ceiling.

He needed this win, not just for his ego, but for his waning career. There had been a hiatus after the last one. People thought he was a loser. Potential clients were afraid to hire him.

Joseph wished for the glory days when he'd first begun the practice of law. Clients practically beat down his door trying to get to him, calling at all hours of the day and night, stopping him in public—in restaurants and theaters—wanting to hire him. He'd coasted for years and grown accustomed to the attention. Other lawyers feared him. Juries were awed by him. Large law firms clamored for him.

Andy's voice startled Joseph back into reality. "Still nothing?" Andy's cheeks were like cherries. The fresh, pink complexion of youth had not yet worn off. His skin was shiny; his blue eyes, like sparkling water. He was a good kid; what's more, he had the makings of being a great lawyer. High energy level. Honest demeanor.

"Nothing." To Joseph, his own appearance was a stark contrast. His cheeks resembled cherries, too. Old, stale cherries, puckered and dried out, wrinkled with age and alcohol. Alcohol.

Andy came over and sat with Joseph. He rolled the chair back and forth, bumping the table occasionally. "You know, Joe, this is the part I hate worst about being a trial lawyer."

"The waiting?"

"Yeah. Shoot, you're used to it. You've been doing it for years. Probably doesn't bother you."

Joseph's hand went to his upset stomach. He thought of the diarrhea he'd have in the morning. His laugh was short, almost rude. "You never get used to it, kid."

"Gee. I thought you'd be beyond it."

Joseph glanced at Andy's face, checking for sincerity. There was another knock in the distance, a loud, harsh one. Had they reached a verdict so soon? When his hands began to shake, he pulled them down into his lap.

Andy's brows shot up; his eyes wide. "Sorry, Joe, but I sure need this win." He jumped out of the chair and approached the doorway again in a few quick strides.

Joseph's stomach gurgled. It hadn't been long enough for a not guilty. He scooted out his chair, glanced at Otis, and walked to the doorway.

The bailiff was coming toward him, another smile on his face.

"They want to go to lunch," he said.

The knot in Joseph's stomach loosened again.

"You lawyers come in here," the judge called, his tall figure in a black robe looming in the doorframe.

Joseph walked toward the man, Andy clamoring behind him.

The judge, his voice rumbling like thunder, advised them of the jury's request. Did they have any objections? It was noon, after all.

"No objections, your honor," Joseph said.

"No objections," Andy said.

Returning to their respective tables in the courtroom, Joseph put on his jacket and beckoned to Otis. Otis stood at Joseph's side, the newspaper now in a tight little roll as he twisted it around and around. Joseph said, "Put the paper down."

The jury came in; their faces solemn. Joseph tried to peer into their eyes, but they wouldn't meet his. The judge advised them not to discuss the case during lunch and recessed until one-thirty. The jurors followed the bailiff who, Joseph knew from years of past experience, would take them to a cafeteria not three blocks from the courthouse.

Otis left. Andy went to lunch with some other lawyers who had been waiting outside for him. The judge was meeting another judge. The court reporter was meeting another court reporter. The secretary said she had some errands to run. The clerk went back to her office. Joseph was left alone.

In the old days there had always been someone who wanted to eat with him, often two or three. They would buy his lunch and pick his brain.

Joseph drove to a small soup and sandwich shop where he bought a tuna on rye and a glass of milk. Neither his stomach nor his wallet could tolerate fancy lunches anymore. He should be watching his cholesterol, but he thought the milk might calm the churning. On the way back, he picked up a magazine to help pass the time.

By one-thirty, the jurors were back deliberating. The judge was in chambers. The secretary was typing. The court reporter was in his office telling jokes to anyone who wanted to listen. Otis stood at the window once more.

Joseph sat in a small conference room behind the secretary's office. He tried to bury himself in the contents of the magazine.

Andy paced up and down the hallway like a caged tiger.

Joseph turned to the second article and read it. And the next.

Then, three sharp raps. He sat up straighter.

The bailiff came around from where he'd been sitting, keys jangling, eyebrows raised. The door clicked when it opened. Words were exchanged. He returned with a note. Smiled again.

"Break time."

"Oh, Jesus ..." Andy said in a whisper. "This is killing me."

Joseph shrugged. He wouldn't admit he felt the same.

A sharp stab attacked his stomach. He flipped through the remaining pages of the magazine and threw it down. He wanted to start smoking again. Sitting in the hard, plastic chair, he watched as Andy continued pacing.

Sometime later there came another knock.

Then three sharp ones. Was that the signal? He and Andy maintained their positions. The bailiff passed them by again, the door latch clicked, voices muttered, then the door closing again. The bailiff returned. Another smile. Joseph wanted to knock that smile to the other side of his face.

"Question," the bailiff said. He went into the judge's chambers. Joseph and Andy stood outside the door close enough for the judge to see them.

The judge's rumbling speech began, "Can the jury have the part of the testimony read back that has to do with—"

The judge read on. Joseph's stomach turned upside down. Their question didn't sound favorable.

The judge called for the court reporter. He read the message again.

Carl rolled his eyes. "I'll see if I can find it, Judge."

Joseph sat on the sofa to the judge's right. Andy sat on the wooden chair to the judge's left.

"Must be a conscientious group," the judge mumbled and cleared his throat. He sat back in his chair and looked from one to the other of them.

"Doesn't sound good for your side," he said to Joseph.

Joseph's head throbbed. The muscles in the back of his neck were stretched tight as harp strings. Their eyes met, and he shook his head. "No, sir."

Andy's torso hung over his knees as he stared at the floor. The silence was broken only by their breathing.

Carl poked his head back through the door. He held the slim white paper on which his machine printed his notes. "Think I've got it, Judge." He read back what a witness had said.

The judge nodded. "Have the bailiff bring in the jury."

They returned to the courtroom.

Joseph and Otis faced the jurors. One woman's eyes met Joseph's; then she quickly averted them.

"Be seated," the judge said. He read the note into the record. Carl took it down with a few swift strokes.

Carl circled around to the witness stand. He read from his previous notes, speaking slowly into the microphone. When he finished he glanced at the judge.

The judge looked at the jurors. "That what you people wanted to hear?"

The presiding juror stood. "Yes, sir. Thank you."

The twelve stood together and left the box. The judge stepped down from the bench and exited through the door to his chambers. Carl stepped down from the witness stand and went to his machine, making a couple of strokes.

Joseph sighed. His eyes met his client's. He shrugged. The wait began again. Andy resumed his pacing. This time he walked in front of the bar.

Joseph rested his aching head on the back of his chair and closed his eyes, his legs stretched out before him, his hands in his lap. His breath did not come easily. The air was still and warm. He urged himself to relax. He thought of his children. He'd get to visit this weekend.

If she'd let him.

If they didn't have anything else planned. Football season was over. That excuse was lame. Maybe they'd missed him enough to overcome her objections. If he could scrape a few dollars together, maybe she wouldn't be so vehemently opposed. He could buy a few hours with them with child support. Blood money. It was practically so, the way she behaved. She didn't believe the dam was stopped up. She insisted he was stingy and selfish and refused to pay out of meanness. Reasoning was impossible. Explanations were useless.

Yes, he understood that teenagers were expensive, but he couldn't give her what he didn't have. No, he wasn't spending it on women, on that woman, that was over long ago, almost as soon as it started.

No, he wouldn't drink while they were with him. Didn't she know one death was enough? But she didn't believe him. She was unforgiving.

His thoughts wandered some more, searching for things more pleasant. He listened to Andy's footsteps. The clock on the wall ticked. The building creaked. Someone sighed.

Another tap, tap, tap in the distance. The footsteps stopped. His stomach burned. Slowly, expectantly, he forced his eyes open and sat up, turning to the doorway. The bailiff waved a piece of paper at them, the sadistic smile on his face again.

Joseph followed Andy to the judge's office. "Another question," the judge said. The ritual was repeated. The jury came in; the jury went out.

Joseph sank back into his chair. Otis left for a smoke. The professional spectators, the retirees who observed out of boredom, wandered in and out.

"You lawyers come in here." The judge stood in the passage, beckoning, his black robe flowing around him.

At their approach, he turned, and they followed him into his chambers.

"It's almost five o'clock. I'm going to let them go home and start fresh in the morning. Any objections?"

Neither of them objected.

"I'm going to write them a note asking them if that's what they want to do. I don't like to drive home too much after dark," the judge said, one bushy eyebrow arched as if daring them to comment.

"Fine, your honor," Joseph said.

Andy nodded. The judge scribbled on a slip of paper. He hollered for the bailiff. The bailiff disappeared with the note.

Back in the courtroom, the judge gave more instructions about not discussing the case. The day was over.

Joseph drove to his apartment, the light drizzle making it hard to see the stripes on the street in the twilight.

He microwaved a frozen dinner, ate it, and sat in front of the TV until he fell asleep. In the middle of the night, he awoke and went to bed. He was up and down many times. Head still pounding. Stomach still flip-flopping. Dreaming of the jury, the verdict. Tossing down more antacid, this time in liquid form.

In the morning, they resumed their vigil.

Andy said, "I don't care anymore. I'm not going to let it get to me today."

Joseph knew he was lying. He didn't reply. He watched Andy pace again.

Joseph rubbed the muscles in his shoulders. Then his neck. He began doodling again. He wanted to do something. Even though he knew he wouldn't be able to concentrate on it, he would read the newspaper when Otis got through. He would write a letter if he had someone to write to, but he didn't.

Another rap, rap, rap.

The bailiff went down the hall, feet scuffling, keys jangling.

Andy and Joseph stood around the corner.

The bailiff returned. Another note. Another smile.

"More refreshments," he said.

"Christ!" Andy slammed his fist into the wall. He re-entered the courtroom. Joseph followed. His stomach felt like someone had set fire to it. He shook his head at Otis.

The courtroom was filling up with people. A prosecutor. A defense lawyer. Another client. The clerk came in and sat down in her box. A plea, she said, her eyes dancing.

Joseph and Andy moved their briefcases to the small conference room, then went out into the hall to wait. Otis was down by the elevator. They watched people and exchanged false pleasantries.

The side door to the courtroom opened. The bailiff leaned his head out. He crooked his finger at them. He smiled one last time. "They've reached a verdict."

Joseph's stomach felt hollow. There was an emptiness at first, and then a feeling that something had eaten him out inside. He signaled to Otis. They went inside. They waited until the plea was done. The other lawyers cleared out. The judge remained on the bench. The clerk stood up in the box as the judge ordered the bailiff to bring in the jury.

The jurors, each of them, stood until the last one entered the box and reached his chair. Then they sat.

The judge said, "Ladies and gentlemen, the bailiff informs me that you have reached a verdict."

The presiding juror, a short, bald, bespectacled man got to his feet and said, "We have, your honor."

"Would you hand it to the bailiff, please?"

The bailiff stepped forward and took the papers from the man. He crossed over to the bench and handed them to the judge. The judge turned to the last page and glanced over it, nodding. He handed the papers to the clerk.

Joseph reached out and squeezed his client's arm.

"Will the clerk please read the verdict?" the judge droned.

Joseph looked over at Andy and mouthed the words, "This is hell, isn't it?" Andy arched one eyebrow and nodded, a huge shit-eating grin on his face.

The clerk cleared her throat, glanced down at the last page, glanced back up at Joseph, and down at the paper again. She said, "We, the jury, find ..." She paused and stared at him.

Something strange was happening, only Joseph wasn't privy to it. His eyes shifted to the judge who wore a devilish grin. Realization struck Joseph like a dagger to his gut. He screamed in torment.

"And lastly, ladies and gentlemen of the jury," Joseph cocked his head to one side and frowned, then shook himself, trying to rid himself of the feeling of deja vu. "I want to thank you for your attentiveness during my summation this morning and throughout the duration of the trial..."

This piece is based on a real event that occurred during my twelve years on the bench.

A LITTLE GIFT FROM HEAVEN

"Leukemia! Oh my God!" Grace Jolivet grabbed her stomach. It hurt like someone had punched her. She felt her husband's arms clutching her and vaguely heard him saying something to Arthur Waller, their long-time friend and family doctor. No wonder Arthur had called them back so quickly. He must have suspected it that morning.

How could their daughter have leukemia? No. She shook her head. It couldn't be true. Not her daughter. Not her baby girl she'd waited so long for. It couldn't be true. Kay was about to graduate and go to college. Her whole life was ahead of her. All Grace could think was no, no, no, no, no.

"Take a drink of water," Roger said, pulling at her hands. Grace opened her eyes to a paper cup in Roger's hand. She didn't want water. She wanted to be told that it wasn't true.

Sitting up straighter, she looked at her husband's grim face. His eyes were teary. He held the cup to her mouth. She grasped his shaking hand with both of hers. Taking a sip, she swallowed and ran her tongue around her mouth. She had to try not to break down. She took another sip and pushed the cup away. When she raised her eyes, Arthur sat across from them and stared at her, more solemn than he had been when they'd entered his office.

She whispered the word. "Leukemia?"

He nodded. "Are you going to be all right?"

She shook her head. "No." Tears came to her eyes, and she covered her mouth with her hand. After a few moments of staring back, Grace pulled her hand away. "Is there anything you can do?"

"There are a few things we can try. It would have been better if we'd caught it earlier."

"I didn't know—"

"Of course you didn't, Grace. No one's blaming you."

"Why don't you just tell us what we can expect, Arthur," Roger said in a trembling voice. He scooted his chair over and slipped his arms around Grace.

Arthur sighed. "I've been doing some reading, and I've already consulted with a specialist. The kind of leukemia that Kay has doesn't respond well to drugs. Chemotherapy can induce a lengthy remission, but it's a complicated procedure and not one hundred percent reliable."

"Is there any cure, Arthur?" Grace asked. Arthur's eyes met hers.

"Not really. A long period of remission is the best we can hope for."

Grace closed her eyes as the room seemed to go topsy-turvy. Roger tightened his grip on her. Leaning her head on his shoulder, she picked up his scent. It used to be reassuring. She felt the warmth of his body through his shirt. She wanted to melt into him. Wanted him to make everything all right.

"It's like this: we do a total irradiation to destroy the leukemic cells as well as Kay's bone marrow cells. Then we do a bone marrow transplant. There've been good results with patients under thirty-five lately."

"But who'd be the donor?" Roger asked.

"They've made a lot of progress in that area, too. Used to be that the donor had to be a twin, later the technology allowed for the use of a sibling's bone marrow."

"But you know Kay's adopted, Arthur!" Grace shook her head.

He held his hand up to stop her from going on. "I know. The experts say that tissue typing has become so sophisticated even siblings are not necessary anymore. We may be able to find a bone marrow donor from the general population."

"May?" Roger asked.

"It's still a long shot. The search could take a while, but—" His eyes darted from one parent to the other.

"But what, Arthur?"

“Well, Roger—Grace—if you could locate her birth mother...”

When they reached the house that afternoon, Grace entered Kay’s room. “Darling, are you awake?”

Roger was just behind her. He pulled Kay's desk chair over and put it next to the bed for Grace.

Kay opened her eyes. "Mommy? Daddy? I was dreaming." Her voice had that slow, sleepy quality to it. She looked at her parents’ faces. "What did the doctor say? Is it mono? Am I going to have to miss a lot of school?"

"Looks like the volleyball team is going to have to figure out a way to win without you," Roger said.

Grace felt the warmth of him behind her. She reached back and he grasped her hand. They hadn't really discussed who would tell Kay. On the way home they'd decided it was only fair that they be completely honest with her, but somehow their conversation didn't extend to which of them would break the news.

Grace knew that Roger was barely holding on to his sanity. She would have to be strong for both of them. They had two problems, the leukemia and the birth mother. She recalled their discussions right after the adoption and Roger's fears that someday the birth mother would return and take away their little girl. Was that what Roger thought now? Oh, they really needed some time to talk this out, but there wasn't any. She felt Roger's hand slip to her shoulder and give it a squeeze. Reaching up, she patted it. She'd do this thing—she'd take responsibility for it, knowing that he was in such pain.

"How are you feeling this afternoon? Any worse?"

Kay's long, dark hair was draped over her pillow as if she'd arranged it on purpose for effect. Her eyes were droopy as she peered out at them from under the blanket she'd pulled up past her chin. "Just very tired." She turned onto her side near the edge of the bed, facing them. "Why are you both staring at me?"

Grace drew a deep breath. There wasn't an easy way. She put her hand to her mouth as if to stop everything from rushing out at once. She would be strong. For Roger's sake. For Kay's sake. "We have to tell you something, darling girl."

"Okay, Mommy." Her eyes went to Roger.

Leaning forward, Grace brushed some tendrils of hair from Kay's face. Her daughter looked so sweet, so angelic. "It's not mono, dear." Grace studied Kay. "You're much sicker than that."

"What is it, Mom?" Her eyes searched Grace's face.

Grace held onto Roger's hand for dear life.

"Leukemia." She bit her lip.

"Leukemia?" Kay's eyes opened all the way. "I have leukemia?"

Nodding, Grace said, "Yes, darling."

Kay's eyes darted from one parent to the other. She closed them for a few seconds and then looked from Grace to Roger again. "Could I have a drink of water? My mouth is so dry."

"I'll get it." Roger hurried out the door.

Grace stared at Kay, remembering her as a baby. She'd always felt Kay had been heaven sent. She'd been an ideal baby and a wonderful child. Every detail of Kay's activity as she had grown up was imprinted on Grace's brain.

"Am I going to die, Mommy?"

"I don't know. The doctor will do everything he can. That's some of what Daddy and I need to talk to you about."

They stared at each other in silence. Roger returned with a tall glass of ice water. Helping Kay sit up, he cupped his hands beneath the glass as she took long gulps. "Thanks, Daddy."

"Let me fix your pillows," Grace said. She eased the pillows out from behind Kay and fluffed them. She needed something to do. Everything seemed unnatural. Stilted. Talking to Kay was suddenly like talking to a stranger. The conversation was awkward. How do you tell someone they might die? She wasn't equipped for this. She never thought she'd have to do this. She was like every other mother who thought she'd die first.

Roger took the glass from Kay and held it between his hands as though absorbing her fingerprints. He looked beaten, with his ashen face and now-prominent gray hair. His eyes lacked luster, like Kay's. If there was a time Grace had to be strong, it was now.

"We had a long discussion with the doctor, Kay. He's already consulted a specialist, but we'll have to take you to see him. His name is Dr. Maitlin. He's got a very good reputation."

"A specialist in leukemia?"

"Yes. There are all kinds of things they can do these days. Do you want to hear about it now? We could let you rest and talk some more this evening," Grace said. She glanced at Roger. He was still holding the glass of water. His knuckles were white. She knew he didn't want to contact the birth mother, but they had to. It was their best chance. And Kay had a right to know.

"What things?"

"Well, I'm not sure I understand how it actually works, Kay, but a bone marrow transplant." She scrutinized her daughter's face. If it looked like the news was upsetting Kay too much, Grace would put the discussion off until later, but, she thought, if it was her, she'd want to know if there was anything they could do. "They find someone with blood as near your own as possible and that person is the donor. In your case, since you were adopted and have no known sisters or brothers, they'll take a blood sample and try to find someone anywhere in the country—"

"What about my mother?"

A sharp pain struck Grace in the stomach. Her hand flew to her mouth. The old insecurities returned.

"My biological mother," Kay whispered. "The one who had me. We'd have the same blood, wouldn't we?"

"Maybe," Roger said.

Grace wrapped her arms around Kay. "You know your father and I love you with all our hearts, don't you? We couldn't love you more if you did come out of my body."

"I know." Kay reached for her father and gave him a hug. She sighed. "This is all so much to think about."

"Of course it is."

"You are going to look for her though, aren't you? I can see it in your faces. That's why you're so worried."

Grace smiled. "If only that were true, darling. The whole thing is what has us worried, but yes, we're going to search for her. Is that all right with you?"

Nodding, Kay said, "I don't want to hurt you, Mommy, but lately I've been wanting to find her. I didn't tell you before, but don't you think that's just a natural feeling for an adopted kid to have?"

"Yes, I do. I don't think you'd be normal if you weren't curious about her—and about whoever fathered you, too."

"That doesn't mean I don't love you and Daddy."

Grace glanced at her husband again. He was holding up. "We know that, dear."

"But Kay," Roger said, "there's no guarantee she'll have the same blood as you. And there also is no guarantee that she'll want to see you, or if she does, that she'll be willing to be a donor."

Kay licked her lips and reached for the glass of water. "I know. But it's worth a shot."

The race was on. They took Kay to the specialist, Dr. Maitlin, who ran more tests. He was utilizing all of his connections to locate a donor from the general population of the United States. Computers were wonderful, he said. Without them, there would be no hope that they'd ever find one in time. The disease was of a type that progressed rapidly.

In the meantime, Grace and Roger went to a family law attorney. Marian Westover was a tall, blond woman of about thirty. They explained the importance of locating Kay's birth mother as quickly as possible.

The next day, Grace accompanied Marian to the courthouse where they were going to present a formal motion to the judge to open the adoption file. Marian had explained that the opening of sealed adoption files was discretionary with the judge. Every judge had different opinions about it. She had explained to Grace that it wasn't necessary for her to come to court, but Grace had insisted. If the judge said no, Grace was prepared to get down on her knees and beg.

First, they went to the clerk's office where the files were kept. Even though Grace told her that she was the adoptive mother, the clerk refused to admit there was a file. The very existence of a file was confidential, and no one was allowed to know about them or what was in them without the judge's approval, she said.

The judge was on the bench. The court coordinator explained that the judge sometimes did open the files, but not if the adopted children were under eighteen. Still, Grace waited and prayed. Finally, the court coordinator said, "You can go in now, Marian."

Grace jumped to her feet.

"It might be better if you waited out here," Marian said. "I'll call you if the judge wants to talk to you."

Grace nodded and moved to Marian's chair, where she could see into the judge's chambers. She caught herself chewing on the inside of her lip. What if the judge said no? What would they do? The lawyer who had handled the adoption seventeen—almost eighteen—years earlier was dead, and no one knew what had happened to his files.

As Marian headed toward the doorway, Grace saw the judge. It was a woman. She was unfastening her robe. She stood in the entrance for just a moment and stared at Grace with steel gray eyes and then she was gone. Grace could feel her heart beating in her throat. She bowed her head and prayed. Surely a woman would understand. To the court coordinator she said, "Ma'am?"

"Yes?"

"Could you tell me, is the judge a mother?"

The court coordinator smiled. "Yes."

"Thank you, God," Grace whispered under her breath.

After Grace waited for what seemed like several lifetimes, the clerk came in. This time she was friendlier. She nodded at Grace and said hello to the court coordinator. "The judge called for this file," the clerk said and went into the judge's chambers.

Grace bit her lip. She felt an ache and noticed that her hands were clasped together so tightly that her fingernails had dug into her skin. She looked at the court coordinator who nodded. Grace felt tears come to her eyes as she silently praised God.

A few minutes later, a smiling Marian came back through the doorway. The judge followed her. She was tall and stout, and Grace had the feeling that few people ever crossed her. She held out her hand.

"Good luck, Mrs. Jolivet."

"Thank you, your honor," Grace said as she shook the judge's hand. She thought the expression on the judge's face was melancholy. "Thank you very much."

On their way to the elevator, Marian said, "I'm going to drop you at home and run to the Twin Cities courthouse. That's where she was from."

"What was the birth mother's name? Can you tell me that, Marian?"

Marian held the elevator door for her. "Go ahead." As they stared at the numbers over the doorway, Marian said, "That wasn't our agreement. I want to, but I promised the judge that I'd be the intermediary." She slipped her arm about Grace's shoulders and squeezed. "If we're lucky, you'll know soon enough."

"You're right. Having you do this just somehow makes me feel so helpless."

"I know, but I promise I'll do everything in my power every single day until we find her."

Having taken a leave of absence from work, Grace let the cleaning lady go and filled her days with tending to Kay and cleaning house. The cleaning helped keep her busy. Each day she picked up around the house until it was neat, and then did a major cleaning job. One day it was the windows, inside and out, including the tracks. One day, it was the walls and woodwork.

Several days had gone by when she received word from Marian.

"I've found her," Marian said. "I've even talked to her."

Grace felt tremendous relief, and at the same time, a sense of trepidation. "What'd she say?"

"She's great! She'll meet with you all and be tested and everything!"

Grace closed her eyes and said a small prayer. "Thank God. That was awfully quick, Marian."

"Yes, we were lucky."

"What did you say to her?"

"Oh—I said I was a lawyer and that I wanted to talk to her about an incident that happened to her approximately seventeen and a half years ago. She said, and I quote, "Thank God. I've been waiting for this call for over seventeen years."

Grace felt a chill. Goosebumps rose up on her arms.

"Grace?"

"I'm here."

"She sounded very nice."

"I'm glad."

"She can't come down here until early next week though. She just can't get off work until that time, and she wants to bring her husband, her mother and father, and her daughter. Will that be all right?"

Her daughter. So the woman had been blessed with another daughter. Somehow Grace was relieved to hear it and at the same time, happy for the woman. She chewed on her lip. Roger might not like it, but it was okay with her if they all came down. "Let me talk to Roger, okay Marian?"

"Sure, call me back."

"Wait. Marian. What's her name?"

"Carol. Carol Dundy. Her husband's name is Mark and her daughter's name is Patricia."

"That was the same name she'd given Kay before we adopted her."

Marian nodded. "I know. She told me."

When the day of the meeting of the families rolled around, Kay was very weak. She wanted to meet Carol in the den, so Grace bundled her up and Roger carried her downstairs. It was snowing outside, and they had the furnace going full force. They didn't want to take a chance that Kay might catch a cold.

The den could be closed off from the rest of the house. Kay had asked her parents to give her a little time alone with "Mrs. Dundy" as she'd begun calling her in the days after Marian's phone call. But first she wanted everyone to meet each other. Nervous, Kay had asked her mother to help her apply makeup and do her hair.

The three of them sat in the den with the television blaring, none of them really watching, all of them waiting for the doorbell to ring. Grace kept studying Roger. She knew he felt as insecure as she did. She knew he thought he might lose the affection of his little girl.

Although they'd been waiting for it, when the chimes rang the three of them visibly flinched. Roger and Grace bounced out of their chairs as if they'd been stuck with a cattle prod.

"Wait!" Kay called out as they neared the door. Both parents did an about-face.

Kay was reaching out toward them. "I want both of you to know that I love you very much."

Grace felt like blubbering. She crossed the room quickly and hugged her daughter. "We love you, too. More than anything in the world."

Roger leaned down and kissed his daughter on the forehead. "Now, how did you know that that's exactly what we needed to hear?"

"Don't worry, Daddy," Kay said. "No one could ever take your place."

Grace smiled at her husband. He was repeatedly swallowing like he did when he tried not to be emotional. She squeezed his hand.

Kay was sitting like a princess on a throne. A very weak, sick little princess, with her hair draped around her shoulders and her blue eyes shining.

Roger cleared his throat as they approached the front door. He peered through the peephole. "It's her."

"Of course it's her. Open the door." Grace shook her head in amusement, smiling at her husband.

Taking a deep breath, Roger pulled open the door and pushed out the storm door. "Welcome," he said.

The woman who came through the doorway looked so much like her daughter that Grace struggled to hide her surprise. Behind Carol was a young girl that could almost have been Kay at age fourteen, except that her hair was blond. Then came a man with blond hair and deep-set blue eyes. Then a gray-headed woman and a gray-headed man. Roger quickly pushed the door closed behind them, to keep out the cold.

Introductions were made all around and Grace took their coats. They stood in the foyer for a moment staring at each other, and then Roger said, "Thank you all for coming."

Mark Dundy said, "You couldn't have made my wife happier."

Suddenly everyone began talking at once, and Grace led them into the living room and asked them to sit down. She found that she could hardly take her eyes off of Carol and Patricia.

"Would you like something to drink?" Roger asked. "Grace made some coffee and hot chocolate."

There were murmurs of assent as Grace started for the kitchen. "Would you like to come and help me, Carol?"

"Yes, I would," Carol said as she got back up from her chair and followed. "Where's Kay?"

"She's in the den." Grace found herself staring.

"She wanted to meet you alone, before everyone else. I hope that's all right." Grace began pouring coffee into the cups she'd set out on a tray earlier.

Carol took a step toward Grace and touched her arm. "I'm so grateful that you've given me this chance."

Grace looked into eyes that could have been her daughter's. Putting down the coffee pot, she said softly, "I'm so grateful that you're willing to do this." She felt a tear run down her cheek and brushed at it.

Carol took Grace's hands in her own. "I know this must be difficult for you."

"It's very hard on Roger. He loves her very much." She squeezed Carol's hands. They were cold. Looking at them, she marveled at how Carol's fingers were shaped like Kay's. They were older, the aging process had caused some wrinkles, but the shapes of the fingernails, the formation of the hands, the length of the fingers were all Kay's.

"I'm so glad."

"She looks just like you." Grace stared back into the woman's eyes. She seemed to be a gentle woman. Tall, like Kay. Graceful. Soft spoken. Grace loved her already.

"She does? When can I see her?"

Grace heard the plea in Carol's voice. It was Kay's voice. Realizing that the whole scene was as difficult for Carol as it was for her and Roger, she pulled her hands away and wrapped her arms around the woman. Carol hugged her back. Grace heard some small sobs. She thought that terrible memories must be flooding Carol's mind. She released her and looked about for a tissue.

Stepping over to the sink, she pulled a paper towel from the roll and handed it to Carol. "I think you must have loved her very much—to have given her away."

Carol nodded and wiped her face and eyes. She sniffed, then blew her nose.

"Well, let's get this coffee and hot chocolate served, and then I'll take you to her." Grace put her hand on Carol's back and rubbed. "It'll be okay. She'll love you right back."

Carol let out a broken laugh. "I hope so."

As soon as they served the others, Grace nodded at Roger and then led Carol into the next room, closing the door behind them. Kay had been watching the door. She had a book in her lap, but Grace knew that her daughter had not been reading. It was only an attempt to appear "cool" about the whole thing, as Kay would have put it.

Grace sat on the edge of the sofa.

"Carol," she said, "this is our daughter, Kay Jolivet. Kay, this is Carol Dundy."

"Hello," Carol said.

"You look just like me," Kay replied, staring.

"And you look just like me."

"Was it tough driving through all this snow?"

"I would have driven through a blizzard."

Kay smiled. "Would you like to sit down?" She indicated a chair opposite her.

"Yes, thank you."

"I have a lot of questions I want to ask you."

"Kay!" Grace admonished her. "Don't be rude."

"I didn't mean to be—but I do have a lot of questions."

"I'd be awfully surprised if you didn't," Carol said. "And I'd like to hear all about you—if you want to tell me."

"I probably will." Kay looked at her mother. "It's okay, Mommy. You can leave us alone now." She patted her on the arm. "I think everything's going to be all right."

"Would you like some hot chocolate, Kay? And would you like a cup of coffee, Carol?"

"Not just now," Carol said. They were staring at each other.

"Maybe later," Kay said. "I have my water here."

All of a sudden, Grace felt like an intruder.

She wanted to stay and hear what was said, but she knew her daughter wanted to handle it by herself. There were some things a mother wasn't privy to, and this was one of them. She could only hope that later Kay would share it with her. "All right. Let me know if you need anything. I'll be right in the next room."

Kay squeezed her arm before Grace got up, as if to reassure her one last time that nothing would be different between them.

"You have just a few minutes before you have to scrub," Dr. Maitlin told Grace before he left them in Kay's hospital room.

He was talking about Kay's request that her parents be present during the bone marrow transplant. Roger had declined. They had discussed it several times, but Roger just couldn't bear to see Kay in pain. He would wait outside.

"No matter what happens," Kay said to Grace, her speech uncharacteristically slow and soft, "remember that I'll always love you."

Grace held her daughter's hand as she stood beside her hospital bed. "I'll always love you, too. You're such a brave girl. I'm very proud of you."

"Thank you, Mommy."

"Can I ask you something, Kay?"

"Anything, Mommy."

"I've always wondered, why do you call me Mommy most of the time, instead of Mama or Mother or Mom?"

Kay's smile was weak. "Well, Mother sounds so formal. Carol, I guess, is my mother. She gave birth to me." She licked her dry, cracked lips. "Mama doesn't seem to fit—it's kind of southern sounding. Sometimes I call you Mom. I remember that. But Mommy seems right for you. You've always been my real Mommy. You're so special. You're my Mommy, that's all."

Grace forced her mouth into a smile when what she really wanted to do was hug the daylights out of her daughter and sob into her pillow. "You've always been special to me, too."

"I know. And Mommy, I want to tell you something."

"What is it, dear?"

Grace heard the door open behind her. It was Roger. He came up to the side of the bed and slipped his arm around her waist.

"I'm glad I met Carol. Thank you for bringing her to me. I know that was hard for you, but I'll always love you and Daddy best."

Grace felt her husband's hand tighten. "The nurse says it's time to go now," he said. "They have to get her ready."

"I'll be okay, Mommy. You'll see. Bye, Daddy."

Roger leaned down and kissed Kay. "Not goodbye, just see you later." He took Grace by the hand.

Grace leaned over her daughter and kissed her. "I love you so much."

"I love you, too. See you in surgery," Kay said with a weak laugh.

Out in the hall, Roger and Grace held hands as they went down to the scrub room. Carol had been in earlier and had been taken off to be prepped. As they stopped outside the door, Roger kissed her and then said, "You know I'm mad about you, don't you?"

Patting his cheek, Grace smiled. "It's mutual."

"I'll be in the chapel again, honey, and then in the waiting room if anyone needs to find me."

"Okay."

"You're so brave to do this."

"I'm not brave. I have to do it." She reached out and hugged him, squeezing him with all her might. "Go on now, before I break down."

He nodded and turned back down the hall.

Grace went into the scrub room and followed all the procedures as they were told to her. She donned the hospital clothes, not recognizing herself when she passed in front of a mirror. Seeing Carol nearly unrecognizable, lying on a table, Grace had the feeling that she was in a dream—a nightmare. Everything had a surrealistic quality to it. From the people in the waiting room who just a few short days ago had been strangers to her family, to the harsh glare of the lights, the touch of the cool air in the operating room, the smell of chemicals, the masked hospital staff, crisp and efficient as they engaged in their assigned tasks—Grace felt herself struggle to accept it as real, when all she wanted to do was force herself to wake up. How had her life gone from normal—wake up, get her family and herself ready for work and school, work all day, come home, tend to her family's wants and needs—to this madness?

The waiting was endless as she seemed to float in time, and then suddenly her loving, brilliant, beautiful daughter was brought into the room. Their eyes locked. Kay was transferred to a table. A blur of light green activity, and her daughter was hooked up to tubes and bottles. She was allowed one last word with Kay, one last "I love you," one last squeeze of the hand, and then slowly, gently, her little girl fell asleep.

Grace was told to stand to the side. She saw Carol, the woman who had been there when Kay was born. She watched her. She watched Kay. She watched the doctors, the nurses, the others. She listened to what they were saying—what words drifted to where she'd been placed out of the way. An endless amount of time seemed to pass, even though Grace could see the clock and account for every minute. Then unexpectedly, the doctor came over to her. Her mind must have wandered. She hadn't seen him until he was right there, standing between her and the table upon which her daughter lay. He was shaking his head. Looking into her eyes and shaking his head. He pulled his mask down. He said, "I'm sorry."

Grace and Roger, and even Kay, had known the risks. They had accepted the possibilities. They knew the disease progressed at a rapid pace and decisions had to be made quickly. They had made them, knowing Kay might have lived a little longer if the procedure had not been undertaken. All of that raced through Grace's mind as she kissed her daughter goodbye. She hadn't been there when her daughter had come into this world, but she'd been lucky enough to be there when she'd left it. Grace gave thanks for having had almost eighteen years with her little gift from heaven.

I have no recollection of the inspiration for this story.

THE RULES

Larry Ray first noticed Mary Sue when he came home from the university for the Thanksgiving holidays. He and Bobby and Jimmy Joe were standing in line in front of the movie theater ticket booth at the mall on the outskirts of town, when three of the sweetest lookin' things you ever did see came waltzing up full of fluff and loud as could be. There was so much giggling, the boys turned 'round to see just who was causing' all the commotion.

The three girls were standing there just as tempting as all get out—high color in their cheeks, straight white teeth flashing as they laughed, and eyes dancing the two-step in the evening light. Thunderstruck, Larry Ray pushed his ten-dollar bill at Bobby and went to the back of the line.

"Aren't you Mary Sue Potter?" he asked the middle girl, the one his eyes hadn't been able to keep off of from the time he heard the first squeal of laughter and looked behind him. She was a pretty thing. Her shiny brown hair reminded Larry Ray of the way his colt's coat gleamed in the morning sun when he took him out for a run. And the bluebonnets that grew out behind the barn each spring had nothing on the color of Mary Sue's eyes. Her little pug nose went up a pinch or two when he began talking to her, as if she knew at that young age the power she had over a man.

"You know darn good and well who I am, Larry Ray Johnson," she said, her voice throaty with laughter. "We rode the same school bus until your daddy bought you that truck two years ago."

Larry Ray's face turned a might pink, but he kept on, his eyes straying a bit from her face down to the area of her chest which bulged under the ample cover of a cable knit sweater. "But you, uh, grew up since I seen you last, Mary Sue." He immediately regretted his choice of words.

The other two girls, who Larry Ray didn't know, busted out laughing, and Bobby and Jimmy Joe started calling to him to come on, they'd got his ticket for the movie. Larry Ray glanced back at his friends and then his eyes were on Mary Sue again. "Can I call you while I'm home from college?"

Her eyes went to her friends, one at each of her elbows, and they all three sort of giggled again. She shrugged. "I don't know, Larry Ray. What for?"

"Come on, Pal," Jimmy Joe hollered. "We're gonna miss the beginning of the show."

Larry Ray glanced over his shoulder and waved a hand at Jimmy Joe. Turning back to Mary Sue, he said, "I thought I could take you out maybe sometime."

The line moved up and the girls with it while Mary Sue seemed to be pondering an answer. Her eyes roved over Larry Ray's face, and she smiled as they slid down his lean frame. "I don't go out with boys much. My pa's awful strict."

Larry Ray wasn't put off. His friends heckled him, but he had to get some kind of consent from the girl. There was just something about her that got him. "Just lemme call you, okay?"

"You better go before your friends bust a gut," she said.

"Okay, Mary Sue?" Larry Ray edged a step in the opposite direction. "I'll call you, and we'll worry about your pa later."

Mary Sue shrugged again, and then nodded almost imperceptibly. "Only not before nine o'clock in the morning."

Larry Ray grinned, his lips spreading from one side of his face to the other, and he took three loping steps toward his friends inside the cinema. A moment later, he was back outside next to her again. "What's your cell number?"

"Don't have a cell phone. You'll have to call our land line."

He reared back. Who didn't have a cell these days? "Okay, your number in the phone book?" He hoped his parents owned a phone book.

"Yep," she said, looking deep into his eyes.

Something stirred inside of him. He would find a phone book before the night was over. "Okay," he said and dashed back inside the theater. Then he was back again. "You still live out there in the woods?"

"You could say that." Her face held a defiant look.

"Okay. Talk to you later." He ran back inside. After he found his friends in the dark, he watched to see if she was going to come in after him, but they must have gone to another movie.

First thing the next morning, Larry Ray telephoned Mary Sue.

"Potter's," a monotone female voice said.

"Lemme talk to Mary Sue."

"Who is this?"

"Larry Ray Johnson."

"Well, let me tell you one thing, Boy. Mary Sue's still asleep. Secondly, she don't get calls 'til after nine. I'm sure she tol' you that, and thirdly, you identify yourself when you call here, ya' hear?"

Heat rushed into his face. "Yes, Ma'am."

"And another thing, for future reference if need be. You don't ever call her after ten at night neither."

The phone went dead in his hands.

At nine oh three, Larry Ray called back and got Mary Sue on the line. "Whatcha doin'?" His voice caught with shyness. He'd known this girl all his life, least since she started school. Living out in the country so much farther than he did, she was always on the bus before it stopped near his house to pick him and his brother up. 'Course he'd never talked to her much, her being a couple of years younger 'n him. Seems like she was a little skinny thing, too, last time he saw her. Not counting last night. But, whoa, had she changed.

"I was trying to eat my breakfast, Larry Ray. Then I got chores and my homework to do before Monday. What're you doing?" Her voice hadn't lost that huskiness he'd discovered the night before did something to his insides.

"I don't know. Can you talk for a few minutes?"

"Guess so." The phone went silent.

"Think your pa would let you go out with me if I come out there and asked him?" he blurted, his chest tight.

"When?"

"Tonight?"

"No, Larry Ray. He's real old fashioned-type strict. I wouldn't even ask him if you could come by. You don't know how it is."

"Darn, Mary Sue, I gotta go back to school tomorrow."

"I can't help it. That's just the way it is around here. Write me, and then maybe at Christmastime you could come by once or twice for dinner or something."

"You don't mean it. Write you? What's your email address?"

"No email. You'll have to write me a letter."

"Write you a letter? Like snail mail?" He was amazed people still did that sort of thing when emailing or texting was so much faster.

"Well, if you don't want to see me," she said, the tone of her voice wispy-soft, "then that's okay. I understand."

"No. No. I'll write." He could ask his mother for some envelopes and stamps. "It's just it'll be three weeks before I come home for the Christmas holidays and all and I thought I could see you before I left."

The phone was silent.

"Okay, Mary Sue, but I'll call you as soon as I get back to town. Be expecting me."

"So long as you mind the rules. You don't want to get me in trouble with my ma and my pa, Larry Ray, okay?"

"Okay. You take care now," he said. "Bye."

"Bye." The phone went dead.

That afternoon, before the sun set, Larry Ray went by and picked up Jimmy Joe and Bobby for a run to Mary Sue's. His father had told Larry Ray that her pa had bought the place dirt cheap because to ranch, it had to be cleared and no one wants to go to that expense when there was other good land so plentiful in the county. Her pa had never quite cleared it, and no one was sure how he made a living.

Larry Ray pulled the truck up the road as close to the house as he could get it, but before he could even cut the engine and get out, the muzzle of a rifle was stuck up under his chin.

"And just who might you be and whatcha want?" a grizzled voice barked.

Larry Ray was as close to wetting his pants as he'd ever been. He tried to look over in the direction of Bobby and Jimmy Joe, but the pressure on his gullet was just too great, so he thought it best to go ahead and answer the question and let them look out for themselves. "Uh, Larry Ray Johnson come to see Mary Sue," he said, his voice sounding like a falsetto in his ears.

The muzzle poked him a little harder, then the voice said, "I distinctly heard my daughter tell you whatcha had to do before you could come courting boy. Are you slow or what?"

Larry Ray tried to turn his head left to catch a glimpse of the speaker, but it wasn't possible. "No, Sir," he answered. "I just thought—"

"You jest better git on outta here, Boy," the voice said. "You wanna call on her, you do what she says."

Larry Ray popped the truck into reverse. "Yessir." He stomped his boot on the accelerator and twisted the steering wheel until he scraped some bark off a tree, then quick as he could he turned the truck around and headed back out to the main road. What with the twilight in his rearview mirror, he could make out but the thin frame of a grisly looking man with a skinny gray and black beard hanging down over the top of some faded blue coveralls, a rifle dangling from one long arm. There was no sign of Mary Sue.

"What the hell was that all about?" Bobby, who was sitting in the middle of the front seat, asked.

Jimmy Joe uttered a long guttural gust of air.

"Hey, man," Larry Ray said, "I don't know, but I think I just met Mary Sue's old man."

"Reminded me of something outta the Hatfields and McCoys," Jimmy Joe said.

"Well, it tees me off," Larry Ray said. "Where does he come off sticking a rifle in my face?"

Bobby blanched. "Beats the heck out of me, Larry Ray. Why don't we go back and find out?"

"Nah, Man," Jimmy Joe said. "That's not even funny."

Bobby started laughing, but Larry Ray was still feeling a little angry. How could somebody just come out and do something like that to him?

"Aw, forget it, Man," Bobby said. "Let's go up to Les' and get a beer."

"But what about Mary Sue?" Larry Ray said.

"Forget her, too," Jimmy Joe said. "She's probably as weird as her old man."

Larry Ray glanced at Jimmy Joe. "I can't, Man. There's just something about her, you know what I mean?"

"The attraction's all between your legs," Bobby said as he elbowed Jimmy Joe who busted out laughing.

"Y'all shut up," Larry Ray said. "No one's gonna talk about her like that."

Jimmy Joe and Bobby exchanged glances.

"So what do you want us to say?" Bobby said. "Give us a break, Larry Ray. We just had one of the weirdest experiences of our young lives and now you're yelling at us. Git off it, okay?"

"Do what her pop says and follow her directions," Jimmy Joe said, mimicking the old man. "Only stop at Les' for a beer, first."

Larry Ray shot them both a dark look but dropped the subject. He'd do what she said. He'd write her some letters in the next three weeks, but come Christmas, he was gonna take her out and that was all there was to it. Pa or no pa. Rules or no rules. He was gonna see that girl.

Soon as he arrived at the campus, Larry Ray threw his bags on his bed and sat down at his desk to scratch out a few lines to Mary Sue. He was still angry at the way her pa had treated him, and he said so. Then, just before he got to the mailbox, he tore it up and went back to his room where he wrote something tamer.

At the end of the week, he received a sweet-smelling couple of sheets in return from Mary Sue. He promptly sat down and wrote her again. And she wrote back. Man, he couldn't wait to get home for Christmas.

The night he did get home, it was after ten. Larry Ray gave his mom a big bear hug, shook his father's and his brother's hands, and went directly to his room. He couldn't wait to hear Mary Sue's sweet, sexy voice when he phoned her.

"Yes," a voice hissed into the phone.

The hair on the back of Larry Ray's neck rose up. "May I speak to Mary Sue?"

"No 'mount of calling after ten's gonna get you Mary Sue," the raspy voice on the other end said in a tone that sounded like a spitting snake. "Don't you believe in abiding by the rules, Son?"

"I–" the phone clicked in his ear. He clenched his jaw as he dropped the receiver back in place. Her daddy was a real creepola. Must be pure hell living with the man.

Come morning, Larry Ray tended to the horses and helped his dad do some mending in the barn 'til after time to call. He wasn't taking any chances this time. When finally he reached for the telephone, he was confident he'd be able to get through to Mary Sue. Her mom answered the phone.

"Is Mary Sue at home?"

"Yep. This the Johnson boy?"

"Yes, Ma'am," he said.

"Only right to say so, Boy," she said. "I'll get her."

Larry Ray shook his head. They got a lot of strange rules he was gonna hafta learn if he wanted to see Mary Sue. He was beginning to wonder if she was worth it when she came on the line.

"Larry Ray?" There was a lilt in her throaty voice.

His doubts evaporated as soon as she called his name. "It's me, Mary Sue. In the flesh." God, what'd he say something so stupid for?

"It's good to hear you. I just got your last letter on Wednesday, but I didn't write back 'cause you said you'd get in last night."

"That's okay. When can I see you?" When he squeezed his eyes shut it was getting harder and harder to visualize her, even now that he was talking to her.

"Hold on," she said, breathless like. "Ma—Ma—okay now if Larry Ray comes by for a bit this afternoon?"

His breath sucked in, he listened to a muted reply in the background but couldn't tell if it was affirmative or negative.

"Larry Ray," Mary Sue's voice came back at him. "How's about two-thirty?"

"Okay, great!"

"But don't be late. And it's only for a half-hour. You'll have to leave after that."

"Aw—half-an-hour? That's hardly time to say hi."

"I can't help it. That's the rules. My pa'd wallop me if I didn't mind them."

"But Mary Sue—"

"You want to come or not?"

Larry Ray sighed long and hard. Maybe he could get them to change their minds once he arrived. "I'll be there. I'm dying to see you."

"Me, too, Larry Ray. Bye," she whispered, and the phone went dead.

Larry Ray rolled his eyes at the ceiling. Her folks were Neanderthals. But two-thirty was time enough to give his colt a run and visit with his brother and eat lunch with his mom. Everything was working out real good his first day home. He headed to the barn to saddle up.

Along about two, Larry Ray had his boots shined, his jeans tucked down, his buckle polished, his best long-sleeved flannel shirt on, and his hair brushed. He smiled at his reflection as he popped his felt Stetson on his head. Boy was he gonna make a good impression. Taking off down the driveway, whistling along with the song on the radio, he focused on how good it was gonna be to finally see that girl again.

It took the full half-hour to wind his way down the country road, through the trees, and over the bad roads to get to Mary Sue's place. He didn't remember it being that long a drive the last time, but then he'd had his friends with him.

There was a nip in the air, and, except for the oaks, the trees were pretty much bare. In his rearview mirror he could see fallen leaves whipping around behind his truck, but ahead everything was still.

Finally, he spotted the beginnings of the Potter place and the feeling of aloneness left him as he turned up the radio and roared up the drive, stopping the truck at the same place as he did before. His eyes flickered around the area, but no one was there to poke him in the throat with a gun again. Least, no one he could see. Feeling stupid, he wondered if this was some kind of weird trap, but he shook off the feeling as he jumped to the ground and jogged toward the house, which was still a good bit away.

Mary Sue didn't come out to meet him like he half-expected. Larry Ray had to go completely up to the door, knock, wait, knock again, and eventually a dried-up looking woman pulled open the door wide to reveal a curtained-off entry way. The clock just inside on the wall read exactly two-thirty. Larry Ray held out his hand and said, "I'm Larry Ray Johnson, Ma'am, come to see Mary Sue."

The woman glanced up at his hat, and Larry Ray snatched it from his head and tucked it under his arm before putting his hand out again. She took it and shook. Her hand felt like a thick piece of sandpaper, and Larry Ray thought fleetingly that if he didn't do something, Mary Sue would be like that when she got old.

"Miz Potter," she said with a nod, then beckoned at him to follow.

Larry Ray did, and without trying, couldn't help but notice how little light filtered into the place. There was an odd smell, too, but he couldn't identify it.

The room off the entry hall was large and low-ceilinged. Mary Sue was standing in the far doorway, an apron tied around the waist of some jeans, her hands tucked behind her back. She wore a bright red blouse with the sleeves rolled up, and something white had spilled onto the pocket over one breast. She looked good enough to eat.

"Well hi, Larry Ray," she said, her voice loud and bubbly.

"Hi yourself," he answered as he twirled his hat around with his fingers, glad to have something to do with his hands.

"Want to come into the kitchen? We're rolling out biscuits for dinner."

He was disappointed but given the screwy history of the family so far as he knew it, not surprised they weren't going to give him any time alone with her yet.

"Sure," he said and moved close enough to put a hand to her back as if prodding her out of the room.

The smile she gave him was like a sunbeam coming through a hole in a sealed-up wall. It was all he needed by way of encouragement.

In the over-crowded, outdated kitchen, there was flour covering a wooden table that stood in the middle of the room. Half the table was stacked up with bowls and rolling pins and such. The other half had some dough sitting in the middle of it. Mary Sue pulled a thigh-high wooden stool out from under the table for him to sit on, then picked up a rolling pin.

"Y'all have fresh biscuits at your house?" Mary Sue slapped a ball of dough with her pin.

Larry Ray glanced at Mary Sue's mother who was just sort of there in the room not doing much other than watching. Damn, he wished he could get Mary Sue out of the house.

"Larry Ray," Mary Sue said again.

"Huh?" He felt dumb as the rolling pin she held in her hand.

"I said, you have fresh biscuits at your house?"

"Nah, not since Mom went to work part-time." They smelled mighty good. "You make 'em all yourself?" His eyes were glued to hers.

"Wanna taste?" She wetted her lips. "Got some honey."

What was she trying to do to him? "Love one."

"Be ready in a couple more minutes." Her eyes danced.

Larry Ray sat watching as she leaned over and slapped the dough again with her pin, rolling up and down, her breasts jiggling under her blouse. He'd never felt this way about anyone before. He glanced at his watch. Somehow ten minutes had already gone by.

Mary Sue picked up a flour-covered glass and with quick snaps of her wrist, cut out more than a dozen biscuits.

The buzz of a timer made Larry Ray aware of where he was. He glanced around the room. Mrs. Potter still watched him. He smiled at her even though she freaked him out. She only stared in return. He wondered where Mary Sue's sister and brother were. Seemed like she had a sister and brother. The sister was older, the brother, younger. And where was her weird-o father?

"Here ya' go," Mary Sue said as she shoved a plate of buttered biscuits into his hand. She took up a jar with golden liquid inside and spooned out a dollop onto the plate. After she set the jar down, she stood and watched him.

He dipped a biscuit in the honey, bit off half of it, and tasted a flavor so smooth he thought he was in pure heaven. A body like that and she could bake, too? He wolfed down several more, his fingers dripping as he dragged each biscuit through the thick nectar, his eyes on Mary Sue's face and lips and teeth and mouth as she stood in front of him, less than an arm's length away, a crooked grin and flashing eyes revealing her amusement.

Within what seemed only a few minutes, she took the plate and was wiping at his face and fingers with a warm, moist towel and escorting him to the door. Larry Ray, who was feeling about as confused as a newborn calf, was resisting, wanting to dig in his heels and stay awhile.

"It's time, Larry Ray." The side of her breast rubbed up against his forearm as she practically shoved him out the door.

"I only just got here, Mary Sue," he said from the front stoop.

"You can come back again." She cupped her hand up next to her face and waved. "Bye-bye."

He snatched back his fingers, but the door had pinched them on the ends. He tried to shake the pain away as he stood facing the door, surprised. The throbbing slowed after a minute or two, and he looked at his watch. Her pronouncement of time run out was true. Remembering that her father might be out there with him, out there with his rifle, Larry Ray made haste for his truck.

It was the darnedest thing he'd ever come across, but the next visits were, essentially, the same. He could come over, was allowed inside for a limited amount of time, and then bounced back out when the time expired. As he drove back home, he always found himself shaking his head to clear it, feeling like he'd been in a fog. Was this love?

Finally, after Christmas when his time at home was drawing to a close, Larry Ray again got up the nerve to ask Mary Sue to go out. To his surprise, she came back on the phone to say she'd be allowed to go out with him on his last Saturday before his return to school. He couldn't believe his good fortune.

He made big plans for the evening. He would pick her up at seven and take her out for chicken fried steak at Lobo's Down Home Dinin' off the interstate. Then, they would go to Dixie Jack's Dance Hall where there was a band every Friday and Saturday night and meet up with Bobby and Jimmy Joe and their dates.

After that, he'd drive her down by the river for a little while before taking her home.

He couldn't keep the grin off his face as he drove out to Mary Sue's house that evening. They were gonna have a good time out that night. He'd earned it. He'd also earned a little time alone with Mary Sue. His fingers ached to touch her.

Aroused at the thought, Larry Ray tried to concentrate on driving. He needed to. A thin mist had floated up from the ground and was winding its way through the trees. It was supposed to be one of the eight longest nights of the year. It already seemed like one of the darkest.

A dim light shined from the front window when Larry Ray arrived. There was nothing to light the way to the front door except his headlights, which he left on for that reason. He felt an odd, uncomfortable sensation on his way from the truck cab to the door, almost like he could see his own frame outlined by his lights. He didn't like it. He just wanted to get Mary Sue and get the heck out of there. He pounded three times on the door and waited.

A few moments passed by before Mary Sue's mother pulled open the door like the first time, and all the other times he'd been there.

"Good evening, Ma'am," he said after removing his hat.

"Evenin' boy," she said and, opening the door wide, stood back for him to enter.

Larry Ray stepped well into the entry hall, if it could be called that, and waited as he had all the other times. Then as he followed her into the living area, he saw Mary Sue in the center of the room. An aura seemed to surround her.

She was the most beautiful sight he'd ever seen. Her rich brown hair glistened and billowed softly around her glowing cheeks. The blue of her eyes came across the room to greet him. Her smile beckoned at him to come closer.

"Like my new outfit, Larry Ray?" She twirled in a circle for him to admire. She had on red western boots and a long red skirt. Belted over the skirt with a turquoise and silver belt was a red overblouse with a deep V neckline and full sleeves.

This being the happiest day of Larry Ray's life, he wouldn't have cared what she wore, but she looked to him like a basketful of red roses. "Beautiful," he uttered. "Ready to go?"

"All ready," she said as she grabbed her purse off a table and took Larry Ray by the hand. They followed her mother as she led the way back to the front door.

"Good night, Mrs. Potter," Larry Ray said as he held the door for Mary Sue.

Mary Sue bussed her mother's cheek as she passed her by. "'Night, Ma. See you at midnight."

"Midnight!" Larry Ray said as he let the screen door slam behind him. He felt like a little boy who'd just had his hand slapped for reaching into the cookie jar.

"Shhh, Larry Ray. Let's go." Mary Sue ran on her tiptoes toward the light from the truck.

"What's this midnight stuff?" He hollered after her. "We can't do everything I planned if you have to be home by midnight."

Mary Sue reached the passenger side of the truck and glanced around as if looking for something or someone. "Shut up, Larry Ray," she hissed as he opened the door for her and she climbed in.

Larry Ray shut the door behind her and, grumbling, went around the other side to climb in. As he did so, a figure appeared in the light between him and the house. The evening mist swirled around it. Larry Ray scrambled into the cab and locked the door behind him, trying not to shiver.

"There's Pa," Mary Sue said.

"No kidding," he said under his breath as his fingers fumbled the keys into the ignition and started up the truck. He popped the gears into reverse and backed all the way out to a wide clearing he'd discovered on one of his daytime visits. He could turn around more easily without turning his back on the house. He didn't want to let that form out of his sight.

As they drove on down the road out of range of the house, Larry Ray said, "Now tell me, what is this midnight business?"

Mary Sue shook her head. "My pa just said that's what time I have to come in, that's all."

Larry Ray reached across the seat and took hold of one of her hands, giving it a squeeze. My, it was soft. "Did you tell him we're going go eat and then dancing?"

"Yeah, but that don't make any difference to him."

"Well, that's just too darn bad, Mary Sue, 'cause there's no way I can git you home by midnight. Why it takes half an hour just from the main road to your house, much less from Dixie Jack's," he said, glancing at her.

She jerked her hand out of his. "No, you don't understand Larry Ray. My pa will kill me if I don't get home by midnight."

Larry Ray didn't realize how easily Mary Sue got riled. He couldn't see her face in the dark, but her voice had gotten a pitch higher. It wasn't worth ruining the whole evening over. "Come on, Mary Sue. Let's not argue. Let's have a good time. Okay?"

She reached out and groped for his hand. "Just so's you understand how important it is at my house to follow the rules, Larry Ray."

"I do, Honey." He squeezed her hand again. "Now, I was planning on chicken fried steak at Lobo's, if that's all right with you."

"Mmm."

"'Course you don't have to have chicken fried steak," he said. "They have other stuff."

Later, at Dixie Jack's, after each of them had drunk a couple of beers and worked up a sweat dancing the two-step, he and Mary Sue pressed together as tight as could be dancing a slow one when Larry Ray whispered, "Ya' know, I still don't think it's fair for your pa to put that midnight curfew on you—'specially being as how this is my last night in town and all."

Mary Sue's head was tipped back, her lips right below his ear lobe. "I know, Honey," she said. "But he really would kill me if I was late. I like being with you, but...." She giggled then, the beer he'd plied her with having its intended effect.

"How's about us going for a drive down by the river," he said, "before it gets too late." His hand slid down her lower back a little so's hopefully she'd get his meaning.

Mary Sue's blue eyes pierced his. "All right, Larry Ray," she said, her words as quiet as a breeze, "if that'd please you."

Larry Ray tipped his head down, his lips brushing hers. "It would. It surely would." A twinge of guilt turned in his stomach, but he pushed it down.

When the song ended, they went back to the table where Mary Sue picked up her purse and Larry Ray finished off his last long neck before dropping a couple of dollars on the table for the waitress.

"Awful early to be leavin', Larry Ray," Bobby said in a louder than required voice.

"Mary Sue's got an early curfew," Larry Ray hollered as the band started back up. "'Sides, it none of your business."

Jimmy Joe started laughing and pulled his date out onto the dance floor. "Y'all have a good time, ya' hear?"

"Just ignore those buffoons," Larry Ray said, shaking his head at his friends. He slipped his arm around Mary Sue's shoulders as they left.

"It doesn't bother me," she said. "I'm just happy to be out with you."

"Me, too."

"Sure you can drive?" She stood up on her tiptoes and looked him in the eye when they got close to the truck. "Wouldn't want to spend our last few hours together getting you outta jail."

"I'm as sober as a judge," he said and laughed at the old joke. He danced a jig in the parking lot.

"Give me the keys," she said.

"Nah, Mary Sue, I was only teasing. I had what, three beers?"

"Are you sure?"

"Sure. Besides, you're not old enough to drive yet. Don't want you getting thrown into jail."

"Am too," she said, hopping up into the truck. "Turned eighteen right before we saw each other at the show that night in November."

"No kidding. I didn't know that. We could get married."

"Now I know you've had too much to drink," Mary Sue said, reaching for the keys. "Gimme the keys."

Larry Ray slammed the door to her side of the truck and laughed as he ran around to the other side. It was a thought. He climbed in beside her. "Come on over here, woman, and give me a real kiss." There was something about her being eighteen that made him feel a little less guilty about how he'd planned on finishing up the night.

Mary Sue laughed as she scooted across toward him. She put her arms around his neck and drew his head down to hers.

Larry Ray gave her what he considered one of the finest kisses of his whole life. When he came up for air, he pushed her away and started up the truck as fast as he could.

They were silent all the way to the river, the only sounds the very muted ones of her hand rubbing on his blue-jeaned leg and of his free hand wending its way under her skirt. By the time he'd found a spot away from the other early arrivals, he was almost frantic, and she acted like she felt the same.

As soon as he cut the engine, they fell on each other, tearing at each other's clothes. When the frenzy of their lovemaking was over, Larry Ray pulled her skirt over the two of them and cuddled next to Mary Sue, the warmth of her scent and her skin sending him drifting off into a sleepy state. He hadn't felt this good in his entire life, ever. He dozed and awakened, his lips against her temple. The sweet aroma of her freshly shampooed hair filled his nostrils. His lips caressed hers, and she murmured.

Her eyes burst open. She drew a deep breath, gasped, and cried out. "What time is it?" She rose up on one elbow.

"Don't know, Honey," he said. "Cover yourself up and let me look." He flipped on the cab light. "Eleven-thirty."

"Oh my God!" Mary Sue grabbed at the pieces of her outfit that were scattered around the cab. "We'll never make it."

"Calm down," Larry Ray said. "The important thing is to get you home in one piece."

She glared at him, her eyes wide as new moons. "Come on, Larry Ray. Let's get going."

"Hold your horses. Let me get my clothes on first."

Mary Sue clutched his bare arm, her sharp fingernails digging into his skin. "There isn't time. Start the truck and get me home."

"God, Mary Sue, be reasonable." He jerked his arm away and flipped off the cab light. She was beginning to make him angry.

"Be reasonable? Are you crazy? I told you if I'm not home by midnight, my pa will kill me!"

"Yeah, but if I drive up there with no clothes on, he'll kill both of us." Larry Ray busted out laughing as he was pulling his pants. She let out a sob. She held her head in her hands. "Gosh, Mary Sue, I'm sorry," he said, but she was crying so uncontrollably that he wasn't sure she heard him. "If it'll make you happy, I'll hurry." He got his pants buttoned, his belt buckled, his shirt on and snapped down the front; he could do the sleeves as he drove. He pulled his boots on.

"Larry Ray," she said, the tone of her voice one of pathetic pleading. "You really don't understand, do you?"

"I'm hurrying as fast as I can." She could be irritating sometimes. Was she gonna turn out to be the kind that nagged all the time?

Starting up the truck, Larry Ray glanced at his watch and said, "Well, if I speed, we might just make it. Come on, Honey," he said, coaxing, leaning toward her and reaching out a hand to comfort her. "It's not that bad. At the worst, you'll just be a couple of minutes late."

Mary Sue continued sobbing and sniffing real big. "You have a handkerchief?"

Larry Ray pulled a package of tissues out of the console. "Here. Now you dry your tears and hold on, Mary Sue. I'll get you home yet." He grinned at her as he slammed the truck into gear and tore down the dirt road on his knobby tires.

They were bouncing all over the truck. He'd forgotten to fasten his seatbelt and Mary Sue couldn't put hers on until she finished getting dressed. He was watching her out of the corner of his eye as she dressed. She was shaking so violently that he wanted to stop and take her into his arms again, but he knew she'd really bust a gusset.

He snapped on his truck light as they reached the turn off to go to her place, and he glanced at his watch. Fifteen minutes to go. They'd never make it. The conditions of that road were too bad.

"What time is it now?" she asked through her sobs.

"Fifteen minutes left."

"Oh no!" Her face, red from crying so much, blanched.

He flipped off the light and sped on down the road. "Darn, Mary Sue, it's not that bad. What's the worst he could do to you?"

"You really don't understand, do you, Larry Ray?"

"What?"

"My pa...he...you know how you haven't seen my sister around?"

Larry Ray shook his head. "I know. I've been wondering where she got off to. I just keep forgetting to ask you about her. But what's that got to do with anything?"

"Larry Ray, my pa...he uh..." the tears started rolling again.

True understanding was slow to dawn on Larry Ray, but when Mary Sue said those last few words, he felt like he was outside of himself, dreaming, as he pushed the accelerator all the way to the floor. She said her pa was going to kill her. God! And she wasn't just saying it. What had he done?

Five minutes of bumpy bad road went by. Mary Sue had dressed and fastened her seat belt around her. She stared straight ahead; her hands clasped in her lap as if she were in prayer. Even in the dark, even with the tear-stained puffy eyes, she was beautiful. He wanted to speed the truck up, but he already had it going as fast as it would go on that road. Could what she said be real? Had he killed her? Had he been reckless and caused her death?

What was he thinking, he wondered as five more minutes went by. He didn't have to let her go home. He didn't have to let her father carry out his threats. What were they all, crazy? He'd save her from this madness. He made up his mind. He'd marry her.

Just as he was about to speak, she cried, "Larry Ray, turn around!" They were approaching the bend in the road where he could turn around most easily.

"What—why? We might just make it, you know."

"Even if I'm just a few minutes late, it won't make any difference, not to him, so I just won't go back." Her voice had evened out.

"I was thinking the same thing," he said. "I'll marry you."

"What?" Her face might be in the dark, but he could hear the amazement in her voice. "No need. I want to live, but I'm not going to let you do that to save me. I don't think he'll come after me."

"This is the most bizarre thing I've ever heard of...your family, I mean. But I love you. Come here." He pulled on her arm as he swung the truck about in an arc. His arm wrapped around her as he backed up and maneuvered the truck the other way. Mary Sue sobbed into his shoulder. Larry Ray put his foot on the brake and cradled her in both arms for a few minutes while she let it all out. His eyes wandered around in the darkness and came to rest on the rearview mirror. Through the mist, something moved. He shivered and jammed his foot on the accelerator and took them on out of there.

"Any sign of them, Pa?" Mrs. Potter called out in the darkness.

"Yeah, but they's gone now," Mr. Potter hollered back. "I'm glad. I didn't want to put this one down. Wave 'bye at your daughter, Ma."

NEXT TIME

"Do you remember the last time Daddy took us camping without Mommy and it rained?" Brenda asked her big sister as the four of them sat at the dinner table munching on fried chicken. The smell of frying oil filled the air.

"I sure do. It absolutely poured. We had to go out and buy some towels. . ."

"So we could dry off," Brenda finished the sentence.

"And we had to go to a washeteria and dry all our clothes because the tent leaked and everything got soaked," Shirley said, frowning.

Myra didn't say anything, she just kept eating and watching the girls as they chattered back and forth.

Gary piled his plate with more chicken and resumed his place at the table. "It practically ruined our camping trip," he said.

"Yeah!" Brenda said. "It rained from the minute we got there until we left."

"Except when we were at the washeteria drying our clothes," Shirley said. "Remember?"

Brenda dabbed at her mouth with her napkin. "Yeah, that was weird, huh Shirley?"

"Yeah," Shirley replied. "Weird."

"We should have stayed home that weekend," Gary said. "It didn't rain here at all, did it Myra?"

Myra shook her head, smiling inside. They shouldn't have gone without her.

“Sure you can't come this time, Mom?” Shirley asked.

“Yeah, Mom, can't you come camping with us this time?” Brenda chimed in.

Myra shook her head. “Daddy didn't give me enough notice. I can't get off work until late in the evening, and I wouldn't want to spoil this trip for you.”

“We could put it off a week or so, Mom,” Shirley said, looking at her dad.

"No, I'm afraid we couldn't, girls,” Gary said. “It wouldn't fit into my schedule. Mom can go next time.”

“It'll probably rain anyway, Mom,” Brenda sighed.

“No it won't,” Myra said. “It's not going to rain this weekend. You're going to go and have a wonderful time. Don't worry about me.”

“Still, I wish you could go Mommy,” Shirley said.

“I do too honey, but don't fret about it.” Myra looked at Gary who was devouring his chicken leg.

After he swallowed, Gary said, “You know, since you 're not going, Myra, you could finish painting the bathroom while we're gone.”

“The bathroom's finished, Gary,” Myra replied.

“Not the door. It still needs paint.”

Brenda scooted her chair away from the table. “I'm going to go play with Michelle until it gets dark,” she said as she picked up her plate.

“No you're not," Gary stopped her. "You and your sister are going to take the tent down in the backyard and start packing the camping gear. I won't have time to deal with it when I get home from my fishing trip tomorrow night.”

“Aw, Dad,” Brenda whined. “I don't know how to take down a tent. I'm just a little kid. Let Shirley do it.”

"No, both of you are going to do it, now go on." Gary's voice boomed like an army sergeant's order.

Brenda made fussy noises as she rinsed off her dishes and put them in the dishwasher. "Come on Shirley, you're not getting out of it," she called to her sister.

"I'm coming in a minute," Shirley grumbled. "Go on out there and get started while I finish eating."

"Well hurry up," Brenda yelled as she slammed out the back door.

Shirley gulped down the last of her milk, cut a glaring look at her father, and got up from the table. She rinsed off her dishes, put them in the dishwasher, and she, too, slammed out the back door.

Myra and Gary finished eating in silence. They hadn't had much to say to each other since Gary belatedly and off-handedly announced the camping trip a week earlier.

"By the way," he had said. "Did I tell you I'm taking the girls camping next Friday?" Then a couple of days later he asked her if she wanted to go.

Now, Gary rose from the table and went into the kitchen. He pulled open the refrigerator door and took out the bread and mayonnaise and lunchmeat.

"What are you doing?" Myra asked.

"What does it look like I'm doing?"

"If you're still hungry, there's plenty of chicken left," Myra said.

"I'm making sandwiches for my fishing trip in the morning," Gary said.

"Oh. I forgot about that. Why don't you hard boil some eggs to take with you? They're always good on fishing trips," Myra said. *And add to your cholesterol.*

"That's a good idea. Why don't you put a few on for me?"

Myra sighed. "It's been a long time since I've been fishing," she said.

Gary glanced in her direction. "I'll take you sometime."

I won't hold my breath. "It's nice that you can take off like this. I mean to get to go fishing with the guys on Thursday, and then to take the girls camping Friday, Saturday, and Sunday."

"You know me, honey, I'm good Joe," he smiled at her over his shoulder as he wrapped the sandwiches in plastic wrap.

"Yeah." Myra glanced at his dishes still on the table.

"Hey Myra, did you remember to get the beer when you were at the store?" Gary put the wrapped sandwiches into a plastic bag.

"It's in the refrigerator."

"Great. I'm going to help the girls with the tent and then watch some television. Why don't you join us when you finish cleaning up the kitchen?"

"Sure," Myra said to his back as he went through the door into the backyard. "I'll do that."

Myra glanced at the mayonnaise and lunch meat and bread still sitting out on the counter. She shrugged and rose from the table. She was tired. All the overtime was wearing her out. She picked up her plate, and Gary's, and carried them to the sink where she rinsed them off and put them in the dishwasher. She went back to the table and picked up their knives, forks, and glasses, and carried them to the sink. She cleared away the leftover food and wiped the table. She drained the chicken grease into a jar she kept under the sink. When she finished loading the dishwasher, she turned it on.

As she leaned over the sink and scrubbed the frying pan, Myra could see Gary in the backyard with the children. They were putting the tent in the camp trailer. She rinsed and dried and put away the frying pan as they were coming back into the house.

"Well, we've just about got the gear all packed," Gary said to her as she finished wiping the grease off the stove and cleaned the counters.

"That's nice," Myra said.

"Hey, honey, did you get my jeans and tennis shoes washed for the trip?"

"I don't know why you want them washed. You're just going to get them dirty again." Dishrag in hand, Myra looked at him with her most innocent expression.

"Very funny, Myra," Gary said. "You can do the jeans tomorrow night if you haven't already washed them, but I need my tennis shoes for the fishing trip in the morning."

"They're in the washer now. I'll put them in the dryer before we go to bed." She ran water through the dishrag and draped it over the side of the sink to dry.

"Great. I'm going to go watch my show now," he said as he left for the den.

Great. "Girls, run upstairs and take your showers before bed."

Chattering between themselves, her daughters hustled out of the room.

Later, after Myra had completed all the household chores, she eased herself between the cool sheets, thinking how good it felt to lie down. She closed her eyes and tried to relax. She was eager for sleep to come. She tried to think of pleasant things as she felt herself slipping off.

She jerked awake. What yanked her back from the sleep she craved so much?

Gary had slipped his hand under the covers. He was pulling at her pajamas.

"Gary, I'm tired," Myra muttered.

"Aw come on Myra, you know you're never too tired for this," Gary whispered.

"Please, Gary, I was asleep." She tried to roll away from him, but he had hold of her bedclothes.

"Be a sport, Myra," Gary moaned. "I'm going to be out all day and late into tomorrow night fishing, and I'll be gone all weekend camping with the girls. Give a guy a break."

Myra dutifully met her obligation. After a few minutes, it was over, and Gary was snoring at her side.

She lay there wide awake, yet exhausted. Finally, she got up and bathed and climbed back into bed. When sleep came, she welcomed it with open arms.

In the early morning, the space beside her was empty. As the fog in her head cleared, she remembered Gary's fishing trip. This had to be the first time in years he was up before her. She dragged herself out of bed and looked at the clock. Almost time to start getting ready for work. She went into the kitchen to put on the coffee and found Gary sorting his fishing tackle.

"I'm glad you're up," he said. "I could use some coffee before I go."

Myra didn't speak. She put the coffee on. She went to the bathroom, and then out into the yard to get the newspaper, stopping for just a moment to take in the fresh morning air.

When it was ready, Myra made each of them a cup of coffee. She sat down at the kitchen table with the newspaper.

"Looks like it's going to be a beautiful day for fishing," Gary said. "Maybe I'll bring a whole stringer home for you to fry up for dinner tonight."

Myra grimaced. "I wish I could go fishing," she mumbled as he packed his new tackle into his tackle box.

Gary glanced at her as she sat at the table sipping from her cup and peering over it at him. "Not this time, babe," he said. "I'll take you next time."

Myra didn't say anything. Gary retrieved his lunch from the refrigerator. He picked up his tackle box and fishing rods and headed out the door. His truck started up and drove away.

As the roar of his truck's engine faded in the distance, she looked out the kitchen window. "Beautiful day, huh?" she said aloud. She sat back down at the kitchen table with the newspaper and coffee.

A few minutes later there was a splat. Then another splat. Then split, splat, patter, patter. Thunder roared.

She looked out the window again and smiled as lightning crackled in the sky. “Maybe he really will take me next time.”

These are the characters in my Mavis Davis Mystery Series. One holiday season, I thought it might be fun to write a "Christmas" story, especially because I'm generally eating a gluten-free, dairy-free diet and have had some interesting experiments in the kitchen.

THE NOT SO GREAT COOKIE CAPER

"Hey Margaret," Mavis Davis yelled from the office kitchen. "What're the bowls and mixer for?"

"Be there in a minute, Mavis," Margaret yelled back from the front of the building. Traffic sounds grew louder as someone opened and closed the front door.

Margaret hurried down the hall. "I was giving Candy some money to run get something from the store."

"I guess we don't have any new clients today, so you're what, baking?" Margaret was cooking more and more lately, like she thought all of them needed to eat. Mavis loved food but sometimes missed meals when she was working in the field. Seemed like her stomach was always making embarrassing noises.

"No new clients. I guess people don't want to be sneaky right now." She scooted past Mavis into the kitchen, her perfume threatening to overwhelm the oxygen in the room.

"Hey, now," Mavis said. "Is that a comment on what we do for a living?"

"I'm just sayin'. So you want to go find something to do? I'll give you a holler when the sugar cookies are ready." Margaret pulled some clips from the pocket of her slacks and pinned her dark hair back. "Go on." She washed her hands and began assembling items on the counter.

"Cookies? Yum." Mavis stood in the doorway. "Looks like you have enough stuff for a bake-off."

"Just about." Margaret pulled two bags of something out of the small pantry and set them on the counter.

"What's that? It's not that brownish flour I've seen you use before," Mavis said.

"Teff flour and brown rice flour."

"That other brown stuff was okay, if you're really off white—"

"That was stone ground wheat. I don't use that anymore. I'm making healthy cookies—gluten-free." She added another bag to the growing pile on the counter. "This is sorghum flour."

Where did Margaret come up with this stuff? "We don't have anyone with celiac disease around here," Mavis said, glad Margaret had her back turned so she wouldn't see the look on Mavis's face.

"Gluten can cause inflammation in people with arthritis. And don't say we don't have anyone around here with arthritis. My hands have been hurting a little lately." Margaret turned on the oven and pulled two cookie sheets from a lower cabinet.

"Probably carpel tunnel. I may have to put you out to pasture."

Margaret tossed her head. "Ha. Ha. I know better."

As the oven heated up, an acrid reminder of the last thing Margaret had cooked wafted into the air.

Margaret set some other things on the counter. Baking soda. Salt. Vanilla extract. Almond extract. Those looked okay. Mavis inched closer as Margaret reached into the pantry and pulled out still more items. Potato starch? Tapioca Starch? WTH?

"Starch? What's that for? Where's the sugar? You can't have sugar cookies without sugar."

Margaret laughed. "I use organic evaporated cane juice, which is sugar but healthier than white sugar. You'll see. Sweeter, too."

An unpleasant sensation struck Mavis's stomach. Was she getting indigestion in anticipation? "OMG, Margaret. What about the butter?"

Margaret went to the refrigerator and pulled out a container. "This is nondairy butter. Way better for you."

"How can you have nondairy butter? Butter is butter. It comes from cows."

One hand on her hip, Margaret turned toward Mavis. "See. This is why I said go find something to do. I know you have some reports to draft."

"But Margaret, you promised sugar cookies."

"They will be sugar cookies." She put her hands on Mavis's shoulders and spun her around toward the hall. "Now go. You may be the boss most of the time, but I'm boss in the kitchen."

Mavis resisted. "I saw a little bag I think you're trying to hide from me. Did it say flax seed?"

"Flax *meal*." She looked at Mavis like she wanted to clobber her with one of the bags of alternate flours. "Would you just go away?"

"Flax meal. Flax seed. Same thing, Margaret. I'm not entirely a novice in the kitchen. Sometimes I put that on my oatmeal in the mornings. But in cookies? Yuck."

"Whatever," Margaret said over her shoulder, using her body to block Mavis's view of the counter.

Mavis retrieved two eggs from the refrigerator and crept up behind Margaret. “Here’re a couple of eggs. Don’t you always need some eggs?”

“We don’t use eggs in this recipe.”

“Who is we? Are you in some kind of weird cookie club?” Mavis pointed to the mixture Margaret had combined in the bowl. “If you were making real cookies, isn’t this when you’d add the eggs?”

Margaret huffed and dropped her shoulders. “The yolks make you fat.”

“Nobody around here is fat.” Mavis looked at Margaret’s rear end. “Nope.”

We use applesauce and some other things to substitute for eggs in this recipe so don’t worry about it.”

“I don’t see any applesauce. Where’s the applesauce, and is it applesauce with added sugar or au natural?” As if she had to ask.

Margaret elbowed Mavis out of the way. “That’s where Candy went, to get the applesauce. And I’m not even going to answer that last part.”

When Mavis looked over Margaret’s shoulder, she saw something she’d never seen before. “What’s that stuff that starts with an X? Some kind of gum?”

“Xanthan gum. We use it to make the dough stick together.”

“But I thought eggs bound ingredients together You don’t use that in regular sugar cookies because you have eggs, right?”

“Where’d you learn that, high school chemistry? That’s what gluten in wheat does. It makes everything stick together. In elementary school, didn’t you ever mix white flour and water together to make paste?”

“We bought paste at my house, Margaret. Are you confident this strange-looking conglomeration of *stuff* is going to become cookies?” She wasn’t sure she would even want to taste one.

Margaret pulled an apron out of a drawer and turned back to face Mavis, looking like she wanted to knot the apron around Mavis's neck. "Mavis, I swear—"

"I got the applesauce, Margaret," Candy yelled, her footsteps slapping the floor.

"You really are going to use applesauce?" Mavis struggled to keep the look of horror off her face. "I'm confused about what you're going to use that for if that X stuff sticks everything together."

Candy in all her glory, multiple earrings in each ear dangling, charged into the kitchen and set a grocery bag down on the counter, pulling out the applesauce. "Here you go, Margaret."

Mavis took a deep breath. Her stomach made little noises. It was as disappointed as she felt. What the result of Margaret's baking would be was a complete mystery, but certainly not traditional sugar cookies.

"Hey, Mavis," Candy said, opening the grocery bag. "Let me show you what else I have." Pointing to the bowl of dough, she said, "That's not how cookies are made." She pulled out a long, plastic-wrapped roll of sugary dough from the bag. "*This* is how sugar cookies are made."

BYGONES

"Darling," Joan said as she came flying down the hall with a sheet of printed paper in her hand. "Marissa's met someone."

Jonathon looked up from the television where he was watching the Lakers' game. "What do you mean she's 'met someone'?"

Joan dropped to the carpet and sat cross-legged next to him. "Read this paragraph," she said, pointing to a section of the email. "See where she says she's met the most wonderful boy—"

Jonathon snatched the paper from her and pulled his reading glasses from his breast pocket, adjusting them on his face. "Hmmm... sounds serious. His parents are coming to town for the weekend, and she'd like us to have them over for dinner?"

"Isn't it wonderful?" Joan asked. "Our little girl."

"Wait a minute, Joan. I don't like it. She's only twenty. Look here," he said, pointing to one line. "She doesn't even give us his last name. All she says is Kevin. Can't be too serious, I hope, if she doesn't give us the boy's last name."

"Jonny, take my word for it. It's serious. A girl doesn't set up a meeting with a boy's parents if it's not." Joan pushed up off the floor. "What'll we serve? I'll have to go to the grocery for something special. That's next Saturday. I wonder if they drink. We'll have to get some wine."

Jonathon rose and followed Joan to the kitchen. "Wait a minute. What if I've already got plans? I'm supposed to go fishing Saturday."

"Cancel them, honey. You've got to be here. They might be her future in-laws." Joan patted his cheek.

"I can't. It's my charter. I've invited half a dozen other men and contracted for the boat."

"Well, come back in time for dinner, that's all. Don't worry. I'll handle them. What time can I expect you?"

"See here, Joan. Let's put it off until another day. I should be here."

"You're just worried it's serious, Jonny, and I think it is, but it'll be okay. I promise."

"But I don't want her to get married. She should get an education first. What are we spending thousands of dollars on that college for?"

Joan groaned inwardly. The last thing she wanted right now was another argument about money. She should have married a rich man; one who wouldn't complain about working so hard for his child.

She looked at Jonathon. She could have done worse, she supposed, but she could have done better. Her mind momentarily went whirling into the past. What would life have been like had she married the boy she'd been so crazy about in college? Oh—but it was a tumultuous relationship. Probably best ended like it had. Still… one couldn't help but wonder. She heard a murmur.

"You haven't been listening to a word I said," Jonathon grumbled.

Joan smiled and shook her head. "Suppose I call Marissa and find out what this is all about. I'll get their names and time of arrival and find out just how serious the relationship really is. Go back to your ball game." She gave him her best teasing smile. "Go on—we're doing this, don't try to make me feel bad."

Typical reactive father, she thought as she watched him make himself comfortable on the carpet again and take a long swallow of beer, his eyes darting from hers to the TV screen. She went into the bedroom to call her best friend. She could talk it over with Petra and get help planning the menu.

"Sammy, put your mother on the phone," Joan said. She perched on the side of the bed, pencil and pad in hand. "Petra, get this," Joan said when her friend answered. "Marissa has met a boy and his parents will be here for dinner next Saturday."

"Wow, that's awfully sudden, isn't it? I don't remember hearing about a boyfriend before."

"You haven't. She never mentioned him in her letters. Still, I think it's serious."

"Sounds like it. What does Jonny say?"

"What would any father say? She's too young."

"I agree. She should finish her education first."

"Don't go backing Jonny up, Petra. I need your support."

"What does she say about him?"

"Nothing much. I'm going to call her this evening and see what I can find out."

"Why don't you call her now, and I'll come right over. I'll help you plan the meal."

"I was hoping you'd offer."

"Go on, call her. I'll be right there. Bob's watching the Lakers anyway," Petra said.

"So's Jonny. They ought to get together."

"Stop procrastinating. See you in a minute." The phone clicked.

Joan tried Marissa's cell phone, but there was no answer. She scrolled to Marissa's dormitory number and punched it in.

"Marissa Silver, please," she said when it was answered.

"Hold on, I'll ring her room," the voice said.

"Hello," Marissa said, sounding out of breath.

"It's Mom. Hope you weren't busy." She felt awkward calling—like she was intruding on Marissa's other life.

"Mom. I was just thinking of you, wondering what you thought of my email."

"We got it. Your father's somewhat upset."

"That's Daddy for you."

"He's planned a fishing trip for Saturday."

"It's okay. They probably won't get there until late—eight or so. There'll be plenty of time."

"But we don't know anything about them."

"They're swell, Mom. I met them two weeks ago. They came up."

"You didn't tell me."

"I'm sorry. It's all happened so fast."

"Is it serious with this boy then? Kevin?"

"I've never felt this way before."

"And how does he feel?"

"He says the same."

"Oh. What do we know about him?"

Marissa's laugh tinkled into the telephone, and Joan realized how much she missed her daughter.

"Marissa... "

"Mom, he's absolutely gorgeous. Eyes the color of the bay at midmorning; thick, dark hair. Oh, wait until you see him."

"That's not much to go on, dear," Joan said, but the tone of Marissa's voice brought back memories of her own first love.

"He's a junior. Chemistry major. He's going to be a research scientist like his dad."

"That sounds a bit better, but won't he have years of school still to go after he gets his bachelor's degree?"

"Alas, yes," Marissa said in her theater voice.

"Alas?"

"We haven't figured it all out yet, Mom, but we're working on it."

"I'll bet you are, dear. Does this Kevin have a last name?"

"Greene."

"With an 'e'?"

"What?"

"Greene with an 'e' on the end?" Joan's heart fluttered as she asked the question a second time.

"Yes, why?"

"Just wondering. And his parents, what are their names and where are they from?"

"You're awfully curious, Mom."

"Well, how am I to address them if I don't know their names?"

"That's true. They're from Richmond Hills. Eric and Hannah Greene."

Joan's stomach flip-flopped when she heard the name of her former college sweetheart. It couldn't be. Fate wouldn't play such a practical joke. She'd wake up in a moment and realize it was all a dream. Wouldn't she?

"Mom, are you still there?"

"Yes, dear," she answered mechanically. In body only; her mind had vacated the premises.

"What's wrong? Do you know them?"

Joan took a deep breath, trying to recover and be coherent for the remainder of the conversation. "I was just wondering. What would you like me to serve? Do they drink wine?"

"Don't worry, Mom. You'll do fine. Get Petra to help you. In fact, why don't you invite Petra and Bob? They'd make it a lively group."

"Yes, Marissa. I might do that." She had to get off the phone. She had to think. How could this happen?

"I've got to hang up now, Mom. Got to get ready for work. I'll email you before Saturday with more details, okay?"

"Yes, dear."

"You'll manage, Mom. Don't worry. And tell Daddy I love him."

Joan shook herself. "We love you, too."

"Call after they leave and tell me how you liked them, okay?"

"Okay."

"Goodbye, Mom."

"Bye, honey."

Joan replaced the receiver and stretched out on the bed. Maybe it wasn't him. There could be two people with the same name. But two people who were research scientists?

Maybe he wouldn't remember her. He'd better. Did he know their names? Ah, but he wouldn't know her married name. He couldn't possibly know it was her house he was coming to. Would he come if he did?

Did his wife know about her? How much did she know? Would she come if she did? Would he tell her when he found out?

"What are you doing in here lying down?" Petra's booming voice echoed through the bedroom.

"I'm... I'm not feeling well, Petra. Could you come back later?"

"What the hell's the matter with you, kid? You were okay a minute ago." Petra stood over Joan, staring down.

"It's my stomach. Would you mind?"

"Bullshit."

"Quiet, Petra." Joan bounded off the bed and went over to the door, closing it.

"Give. Something's wrong. What is it?"

"I don't know what I'm going to do." Joan tried to cry, but the tears wouldn't come.

Petra stood, hands on hips, waiting for an explanation. "I can't help if you don't tell me, Joan. What is it?"

Joan's eyes searched Petra's broad face for support. "Promise you won't tell anyone? Even Bob?"

"Cross my heart. Now tell."

"That boy's father… "

"Marissa's boyfriend? Well?"

"I knew him in college. We were…"

Petra stared at Joan, dumbfounded. "Oh... my God. You've got to be kidding."

"No," Joan said, sitting down on the bed again, holding her stomach.

"Oh, shit. How'd you find out? Marissa tell you?"

"Marissa doesn't know. She told me their names," Joan said, her voice dropping.

"Jonny doesn't know?"

"No. He thinks I was a virgin."

"Oh, shit."

"You can say that again," Joan said, almost laughing in spite of herself.

"I will. Oh, shit. What are you going to do?"

"I don't know. I could get deathly ill. Take poison. Run away from home. Get a divorce."

"Glad to see you've kept your sense of humor. What are you really going to do, tell Jonny?"

"Do I look like I'm nuts? You know how naive and innocent he is. It would destroy him. Absolutely destroy him."

"Maybe the guy won't remember you." Petra began pacing up and down the room.

"I already thought of that. Maybe he won't, but that's very doubtful."

"It was that serious, huh?" Petra wore a quirky smile.

"Yes. And more."

"Well, frankly Joan, there's nothing you can do."

"I know." Joan cross her arms.

"Be a gracious hostess and hope he's gentleman enough not to say anything."

"Right."

"Pray he doesn't let anything slip to Jonny."

"I am." Her brown eyes followed Petra as she walked.

"If he does, make like it wasn't important—that you forgot to mention it over the last twenty-one years of marriage."

Joan groaned.

"In the meantime, let's plan an elaborate meal that's so good he'll wish he'd married you."

Joan took a deep breath and sighed. Petra patted her shoulder. "There's nothing for it, kid."

"I know. I was just thinking—"

Petra took her by the arm. "Come on, you've got plenty of time for that during the week. Let's go into the kitchen and make like nothing's wrong so Jonny won't get suspicious."

Joan stood up, her knees settling down. "You'll come, won't you?"

"Bob and I?"

"Wouldn't miss it for the world." Petra put her arm around Joan's shoulders and gave them a squeeze. "Let's go."

Joan pasted a smile on her face and went past Jonny on the living room floor. "We're going to plan the menu. Anything special you'd like?"

"You talk to Marissa?" he called after her.

"Yes, dear," Joan called from the kitchen table where she'd sat with her pad and pencil, her back to the living room. She cast her eyes at Petra who was across from her.

"Well, what'd she say?" Jonny asked, his voice louder as he came to stand in the doorway.

Joan breathed deeply, hoping she would sound normal. "It's Mr. and Mrs. Eric Greene. Her name is Hannah and they're from Richmond Hills." She glanced back at Jonny to see if he'd detected anything that would give him the least inkling. His face drew up into a frown.

"Never heard of 'em," he muttered as he looked back into the living room.

"He's a research scientist." Did he hear the tremor in her voice?

Jonny glanced back at Joan, an odd expression on his face.

She didn't know what that meant. "That's what the boy wants to be, Marissa said."

"Oh. And is it serious?"

"Yes, apparently." She looked to Petra for support. Petra grimaced.

"We'll see," Jonny said, then drifted back into the living room.

Joan shook her head.

"I'll never get past this," she whispered to Petra.

Petra squeezed her hand. "Come on. You can worry about that later."

Joan did worry about it later. She had a restless night, but thankfully Jonny was a deep sleeper.

Sunday, she set about cleaning. She started in the kitchen, scrubbing the stove until all the burners shined like new. Then she washed and waxed the floor.

Monday, she gathered up the draperies and dropped them at the cleaners on the way to the office. Monday evening, she tackled the living room and wondered if he would think it shabby.

Tuesday, it occurred to her that she'd gained twenty pounds since college. Would he think her fat and ugly? She'd have to practically fast for the remainder of the week to fit into the blue dress she'd decided to wear. She paid extra attention to the guest bathroom. Didn't want him to think them careless, dirty people.

Wednesday, she received another email from Marissa and ran right out to the liquor store to have on hand what they drank. Then she dusted and waxed the entry hall, so they'd be impressed upon arrival.

Thursday, she changed her mind about the blue dress and dragged Petra to the mall after work. They stayed until closing selecting a new dress that didn't show all the flab, bumps, and wrinkles. She gave herself a facial that night.

Joan extracted a promise from Jonny that he'd cut and edge the lawn on Friday evening. He did so begrudgingly. What was the matter with him? He'd been grumpy all week. While he did that, she made sure the tablecloth and napkins were clean, put the draperies back up, vacuumed the living room again, and polished the silver.

Saturday morning, Joan kept her hair appointment. She was having them color the grey. Thinking about Eric while under the dryer, she felt a moistness between her legs. Nausea rose up in her throat. Disgusting. How could she betray Jonny after all these years?

When she got out, she went to the grocery and made her purchases. At home, she ate a late lunch and then leaned over the toilet bowl and vomited.

The phone rang. Joan lifted her cheek from the side of the sparkling toilet. Who would dare call her at a time like this?

"Hi, Mom." Marissa's lively voice jumped out at her.

"Hello, dear. Is something the matter? Are the Greene's canceling?" she asked, hope suddenly making her feel better.

Marissa laughed. "They wouldn't dare. I told Kevin so. I was sure you'd be working on the house all week."

"Oh, you didn't."

"No, just teasing. I wanted to find out how it's going and tell you not to fuss too much. They've really got simple tastes. They're great, Mom. You'll like them."

Joan rolled her eyes toward the ceiling. "I'm sure I will, dear. Is that all you wanted? Because I've still got a lot to do before tonight."

"Well, I needed to let you know they're running a little late. It probably won't be until nine that they get there. They stopped by here to see us, and I'm afraid we kept them too long. Threw them totally off schedule. Dr. Greene said they're going to spend the afternoon with his mother. She lives in a senior citizen's complex on the way down there. Then they're supposed to have cocktails with some other scientist somebody or another when they get to town. You don't mind, do you?"

Joan sagged against the bedpost. Could she stand the anticipation until nine? "No, that's fine, honey. I appreciate you calling."

"Okay, Mom. Gotta go. Kiss Daddy for me when he gets in."

"Bye, dear."

Joan hung up and then rang Petra. "I've got a short reprieve. Can you come over now?"

"On my way."

When Petra arrived, Joan was sitting at the table, scotch in hand. Petra took the glass from Joan and sniffed it.

"Since when have you taken to drinking scotch?"

"Since now. I wanted to get up the courage to kill myself."

"Don't be silly. It's almost over."

"Give me that." Joan took the glass back, swallowed a mouthful, and made an ugly face. "What do you mean it's almost over?"

"The waiting is usually worse than the actual event." Petra took the chair adjacent to Joan's.

"Not in this case."

Joan took another gulp.

"Ugh. How can you stand that stuff? And you don't even drink."

"I do now."

Joan laid her head on her arm.

"What am I going to do? On top of everything else, Jonny's been in a foul mood all week."

"What do you expect? He's a father. Maybe the fishing trip will make him feel better. I know Bob was looking forward to it." She grinned, her eyes sparkling. "Come on, Joan. It's not the end of the world."

"Feels like it," Joan muttered. "I actually get turned on when I think of him, Petra. Isn't that horrible?"

"Not if you two had a good sex life."

"Don't be crass."

"Is that what's bothering you?"

"One of the millions of things. How can I face Jonny when I haven't told him about E-E-Eric?" Joan drank down the rest of the scotch and reached for the bottle.

"Holy cow. Don't be so melodramatic." Petra slapped Joan's hand away. "You'll make yourself sick."

"I've already been sick. I threw up a while ago."

"Oh, Joan."

"I can't do it, Petra. You could. You're big and strong. You never worry about anything. I can't. Jonny never had another woman but me, and he thinks I never had another man but him."

Her words were beginning to slur.

"Okay, Joan. I'm serious now. You're going to do it. You'll have them over. You'll pretend nothing's wrong. You'll pretend you don't know the man. Everything will be all right, you'll see." She got up out of her chair and went to Joan. "Come on. Get up. I'll take you into the bedroom. You lie down awhile and have a good nap." She helped Joan to the bedroom and the bed. "I'll get dinner started—make the salad and desert." She stared down at her friend. "When you wake up, you'll feel better," Petra said, her voice softer.

"They're not coming 'til nine."

"Okay. That's fine." Petra tiptoed to the door. "Rest now."

When Joan awoke, it was to Jonny's voice coming from the garage. "... caught. Come see. It's the biggest catch in centuries."

She stumbled out of bed and through the house to the garage.

Jonny was unloading his truck; setting the cooler on the floor. He appeared happier than he'd been all week.

"Been napping?" he asked, grinning. "Just look in the cooler." He flipped open the lid. "It's the best catch I've had in years."

"Glad you had a good trip?" Joan peered into his cooler. She was pleased he was so happy. "It's wonderful, honey. But let's get them packaged up and into the freezer before our guests come."

"Bob made pictures. Can't wait 'til they come back," he said.

"Jonny, did you hear me?"

"What?" He frowned. "Oh, that. Missed you today. You would have enjoyed it."

She smiled at him again. "Missed you, too."

He came up to her, smelling of fish, and put his arms around her. "Had your hair done. Looks great." He kissed her on the mouth. "Love you, you know."

Joan's eyes searched his. She wrestled his arms from around her and put his hands together in front. "Love you, too, now that you mention it." She turned back toward the house. "Let's hurry. We've got to shower and dress, and I've got to put the meat on. It's getting late."

"I'm coming. I'm not looking forward to it, but I'm coming."

Joan glanced back. Jonny had a curious expression on his face.

They put away the fish. They showered and dressed. As the minutes passed, the anxiety Joan felt turned into a hard ball in her stomach. How would she ever make it through the evening? What would Jonny do when he found out?

Petra and Bob showed up half-an-hour early. Petra helped in the kitchen. Bob and Jonny sat in the living room discussing the fishing trip.

At precisely nine o'clock, the doorbell rang. Joan and Petra exchanged looks. They hugged. Joan went through the living room and smiled at Jonny who was getting up from the sofa.

"I'll answer it," she said. "Don't get up."

He got up anyway.

Joan peered through the peephole in the front door. There stood Eric Greene under the porch light, almost as handsome as she remembered him. His hair was thinner. His waist was thicker. His eyes were bluer.

Next to him stood a sophisticated-looking blonde. So that was who he married. Joan studied her as best she could for the few seconds she could stall before opening the door. Jonny came up behind her and she smiled at him. "It's them, I think."

He sighed heavily. "Well, let them in."

Joan pulled open the door. Before she could say anything, the woman said, "Jonathon, darling. It's been eons. How've you been?" She threw herself into Jonny's arms.

Jonny's face blanched. His expression looked pained and full of anguish as his eyes met Joan's.

Joan looked from Jonny to Eric and back again. What were the odds? She laughed, shook hands with Eric, received a kiss on the cheek, and took them in to dinner.

Do you ever wonder if we're alone or what it would be like to live in another dimension?

DOUBLE OR NOTHING

She got up from the Sunday Night Movie, leaving James glued to the screen as usual, and went into the bedroom, to her bedside table where she pulled out her journal. She plumped the pillows at the head of the bed and leaned back, getting comfortable, and grappled in her purse for a pen. Finding one, Anna turned to the first blank page to make her next entry.

September 25th

Dear Anna,

Are you there? I've been trying to make contact but again find that I've been unsuccessful. I can't help but feel you're there. In fact, I'm convinced you're there, but I have so many questions. Not doubts, but questions.

I want to think you're just like me. Are you? I've just about got it figured out that you're either on another planet in another solar system, or in a parallel world—another dimension. But I've told you this before, Anna. And I 'm sure you know it, Anna.

Anna, that's a nice name. Your mother had good taste. Ha. Ha. I never realized how much I liked our name until I knew you were there to share it with, Anna.

Do you feel like I do? Are you just like me? Do you have two children? And are there stretch marks on your belly and on your breasts?

Do you know all my questions before I ask them? And more than that, do you know the answers? Because I don't. Here comes James. I'll write again and keep trying to make contact.

Anna

She shoved the book away and closed the drawer. "Is your movie over?" she asked when James came through the bedroom door.

"No." He pulled his tee shirt over his head and went into the bathroom where he urinated in the bowl.

October 2nd

Dear Anna,

I just got home from a meeting where I imbibed quite a lot of beer. I was thinking of you again. Do they have beer there? Do you like it? Surely you must, or I wouldn't. Oh, how I long to talk with you. Do you ever have feelings that everyone is looking at you as if you were an oddball? I do. My mother would say I 'm paranoid. No, that's not true. She wouldn't say so, she'd just look at me funny and think it.

Is your mother that way? Is she just like mine? I wonder if our parents have to be duplicates of each other for us to be. It would be more interesting if they weren't. Can you imagine two totally unrelated sets of genes, in two different dimensions, producing identical people? My daughter says we'd be mirror people. She says I'm weird, but she understood what I was saying when I told her about you. I think she has a similar notion.

Do you have children? Are they like mine? My two daughters, one is thirteen years old and the other, nine, are as different as night and day.

Speaking of that, if you weren't on another planet or in another dimension, but, instead, you were a mirror person, wouldn't we be as different as night and day? Wouldn't we be opposites? I wonder.

Oh, I want so badly to talk to you. Speak to me, speak to me, Anna.

I've been wondering. Are the people there all different colors like here?

I have all this stuff in my mind which I believe, but no confirmation of it.

Anna X X

October 12th

Anna,

I'm so confused. What's it all about? Do you believe in God? Why are we here? To what purpose? What end?

I was watching television this evening and a lady said to a man that she had it all. Her own business, money, position, and that it's all garbage.

What isn't? It bothers me that I can't figure out a justification for my existence, and it bothers me that it doesn't seem to bother anyone else. Why am I here? To procreate? To entertain? To help others? To explore? To experiment? A simple belief in God must be what helps others get by.

Well, for years I've gotten by because I pushed the thoughts to the back of my mind. I try not to worry about it. But sometimes I can't push the thoughts away. I push and push—even pull and shove a little, but for days I ponder. I 'm depressed. I feel worthless.

Goodbye,
Anna

October 16th

Dear Anna,

Do you ever get depressed? I've been going through a lot of depression lately, but I'm not sure what I should attribute it to. I went out the other day and got my hair cut and bought a lot of clothes and that helped some. I don't usually do that. I usually just exist during those periods, and something, I don't know what, comes along and snaps me out of it. This current period of depression, though, has been going on a long time.

A friend of mine told me tonight that she had a dream that something horrible happened to me. She didn't know what it was because when she woke up, she couldn't remember the dream. I hope she wasn't dreaming about you instead of me. But I'd know if something happened to you. I know I would.

I've been thinking of what other means of communicating with you are available to me. If you're a mirror person, then if I leave these pages out, you should be able to read them with a mirror.

If you're on another planet, then I could go outside and talk to you or read this outside—assuming that the sound would somehow get to you.

If you're in another dimension, can you just know what I'm communicating by my thoughts?

I'm not trying to put any pressure on you, but couldn't you do something soon to acknowledge that I'm getting through to you?

Yours in depression,
Anna

October 20th

Anna,

Are you up there writing in your book like me? Are you wondering if there's more to your life? Were you a groupie when you were young?

Or are you not on another planet, but in another dimension? If I killed myself, would I meet you on the other side, a victim of murder with me the perpetrator because killing me was the act that killed you?

If you're on another planet, would our deaths be simultaneous if I chose to kill myself?

If I could meet you, maybe I wouldn't be so lonely. Maybe you really are like me, and I'd have someone who so completely knows my feelings that I wouldn't even have to say them aloud.

Do you, too, cringe when you hear certain words spoken by someone you thought you liked? That happened to me today.

Or perhaps there is no prejudice where you are. But if it is a parallel world, there would have to be. Or still another possibility, what if I got to the other side and found out that you were black? A mirror opposite of me. And what if the whites were the minorities? I'd love it, but it would be too bad I wouldn't be able to bring everyone with me—to experience it. On the other hand, if black was then the majority class, it wouldn't make much difference, would it? That's something to ponder, isn't it?

Love,
Anna

October 28th

Dear Anna,

Are you feeling as utterly useless, as much of a waste as me? Do you sit in a bay window and look out and ask the Lord (or somebody) to put you into contact with me?

If I did kill myself, would you necessarily have to die? Maybe I could find out. Maybe you want to die to find me, and if you kill yourself, would that cause me to kill myself? If I changed my mind at the last minute, and you didn't, would I be forced to go through with it?

What if I got to the other side and found you were the exact opposite of me—-of everything I think I am? What if you were mean and hateful and uncaring? What if I got to the other side and found I'm all the things you never wanted to be? What if you never worry, are never depressed, never spend time thinking? What if your life is worthwhile and you despise me? Oh, I couldn't stand it if I found you and you hated me.

What if you are all the things I'm not—slim and beautiful, have a clear complexion, beautiful hair and nails, and no sagging breasts, no callused feet, no ingrown toenails, no dry skin, no eye infections, no split ends?

Is there hate and fear there? Is there envy and greed and anger? Are there mosquitoes and roaches? What about heart attacks and strokes? Is there old age, disease, and pestilence?

Where are you? Do you have another name?

How can I get in touch with you? Can I leave here and find you?

Anna laid her diary on the jumbled bedclothes. Time to find out. She shuffled into the bathroom, to the medicine cabinet. She took out all the pill bottles. Her arms were full as she approached the bed. She dumped the bottles next to her journal and went into the kitchen for a large glass water. Returning, she set the glass on her bedside table. Pushing the bottles and the book aside, she made room for herself on the bed. She picked up the first bottle, read the label, opened it, and poured the capsules into her hand. She pushed the pills into her mouth and drank after them. She repeated this process until all the bottles were empty, then she scooped them off the bed onto the floor.

Plumping her pillows, she sat back and waited. Would the answers come to her in the minutes or seconds before death? Her stomach began to ache. The pain was tough.

Five minutes passed. Ten.

It wouldn't take them long to find someone to replace her at work. There were a lot of unemployed people out there. A lot of hungry mouths to feed.

James would be all right without her. Probably happier. Her depressions got to him. He would find someone who was happy-go-lucky, someone who doted on his every word. There were a lot of women out there looking for husbands. He'd be snatched up fast.

A stab of jealousy struck her, or was it just a reaction to the pills?

The girls. Would they be okay? Sure. The boy down the street seemed okay, and his mother just committed suicide a few months ago. The other day he was standing in his driveway, laughing and talking with his girlfriend. His mother's death didn't seem to have had such a profound effect on him.

But what was it her daughter had said? How upset the boy's girlfriend had said he was. How he had cried and cried. He missed his mother so badly, she'd said. And how she was glad it was his mother and not hers.

Oh, April and Mary, I love you.

She couldn't do it, couldn't leave her children. Not just now. Not when they were still young and needed her.

Panic struck Anna. The pain in her stomach was growing worse. She was drowsy. What had she done? She'd have to call an ambulance. She looked across the bed. Her cell phone seemed miles away. Struggling, she inched her way toward it.

She grew closer and closer, finally reaching the edge of the bed. She put out her hand and grasped the phone. Pulled it toward her. Reached out her other hand for the buttons. She was so sleepy.

Maybe she should just put her head down and go to sleep. No. Call for help. She punched a button. Nine. Then another. One

"Would you quit?" The voice of an angel.

Anna looked up. A reflection of herself stood beside the bed. "What…?"

The figure reached out and took the phone from Anna, switching it off. "I can't let you do that."

The apparition sat on the edge of the bed.

"Are you…?"

"Yes, and I've got to stop you from annoying me. Your communications have been nothing but pure torture. I'll tell you what you want to know, but that's it."

Anna closed her eyes and listened as the voice continued, giving her all the answers. She was in heaven, she thought, just before she went to sleep.

This story appeared originally in Tidelines An Anthology of Galveston Writers, Galveston Writers Coalition, 1998.

JURY DUTY

It was date rape. They called it sexual assault, but that didn't change what it was. What's more, my old classmate, Bobby Williamson, was the accused, and I had been called for jury duty.

Bobby still looked young enough to be in high school. His rich brown hair had thickened, rather than thinned, with age. His blue eyes sparkled like crystals. Something in my stomach fluttered as I remembered what it had been like when he'd turned those eyes on me in high school. In the recesses of my brain, I could smell the Brut cologne and feel Bobby's hot breath upon my cheek.

A look of recognition crossed his face when the assistant district attorney, Miss Dalton, said to me, "Number five, you indicated that you know the defendant. Stand up, please."

I tried not to look at Bobby, but my eyes involuntarily darted to him. He grinned and whispered to his lawyer. I felt like a slab of meat on display.

"You are acquainted with the defendant, ma'am?" the prosecutor asked.

I nodded. "We were in high school at the same time."

"How well do you know him?"

"I last saw him at graduation twenty some-odd years ago."

"Were you close in high school?"

"How do you mean?"

"Did you hang out with the same people?"

"He played football and baseball. Everyone knew him. I was on the drill team."

He was beaming. His dimples made him look sweet even now.

"You ever go out with him?"

"A couple of times."

"Nothing serious?"

My stomach churned. "We went out once or twice, that's it."

"Your experience with the defendant would make it difficult to be impartial, wouldn't it?" Her face was like a thundercloud.

I smiled at Bobby. "It would be difficult, ma'am, but I could do it."

He elbowed his attorney who wrote something down.

When it was the defense lawyer's turn to question us, he didn't ask me anything. I thought he must know the state's attorney would not pick me. A few minutes later, though, I found myself on the jury.

The prosecutor made her opening statement. "The evidence will show the defendant took the victim to dinner to discuss her boyfriend problems. Afterward, he forced his way into her apartment and sexually assaulted her."

The defense attorney was Mr. Rankin. He told us he would show that it wasn't sexual assault. It was a consensual act by two adults.

"Look at Bobby Williamson," he said to us. "Does Bobby appear to be the sort of man who couldn't get sex without force?"

The attorney for the state called her first witness.

A young woman walked tentatively into the courtroom, head bowed, chin-length brown hair swinging in front of her face. She could have been my daughter.

"State your name," the assistant D.A. said after the girl was seated on the witness stand.

"Julie Dunaway," she said. Her eyes seemed to be focused on the blackboard that stood behind the state's table.

"How long have you been acquainted with the defendant?"

"Since I was a little girl. He taught me in Sunday school."

"Did you go out with the defendant of your own free will?"

"Yes, Ma'am. He asked me to dinner. My boyfriend and I had just broken up." Her hands gripped the microphone stand.

"What happened after dinner, Julie?"

"He walked me to my door." She glanced in Bobby's direction and then quickly away. "Then shoved me up against the wall as he shouldered his way into my apartment...an—and...made me have sexual intercourse."

"On cross, the defense attorney said, "You weren't a virgin when you went out with Mr. Williamson, isn't that true?"

Ducking her head, she said in a tiny voice, "True, sir."

Mr. Rankin asked, "You invited him in. Is that not true?"

"No, sir," she answered. She clutched her arms to her chest as though to keep herself warm.

"You got him inside your apartment and enticed him and when your boyfriend found out, you yelled rape, correct?"

"No, sir."

"Bobby didn't have a knife or a gun, did he? He didn't beat you up, did he?"

"He slapped me a couple of times."

"Come now, Miss Dunaway. In all honesty, he didn't leave a bruise on your body, did he?"

"No, sir, but he threatened—"

"But you weren't *hurt,* were you?"

Later, a doctor testified about the rape kit and the evidence they had gathered. The hair and semen matched Bobby's.

Bobby was a magnificent witness. He was born to play to an audience like a puppeteer to a group of squealing children.

"Were you with Julie that night?" Rankin asked.

Bobby folded his hands on the counter. I thought he was going to say, "Let us pray," but he said, "Yes, sir. I was. It was our second date." He studied his knuckles, then our faces.

"*Second* date?" Rankin turned and looked our way. "And where had the two of you gone, sir?"

"To dinner. A movie. Dancing until midnight."

It sounded so romantic. Sincerity seemed to be written on Bobby's face with indelible marker. How could this angel of a man have other than amour in his soul?

"Did you force her to have sexual intercourse with you?"

"No, *sir*," Bobby said. "She knows she wanted it."

Finally we came to the part where the judge read us the court's charge. "Do not let bias or sympathy or personal experience play any part in your deliberations," the judge said. Later, after the lawyers performed their closing arguments, Bobby winked at me as we filed out of the jury box. I smiled at him.

We voted. We argued. The room grew hot. Later, it was cold. We sent the bailiff for coffee. We voted again. It was still not unanimous. Everyone knew where everyone else stood. We returned from lunch. We argued and discussed. Finally, it *was* unanimous.

When we went back into the courtroom, Bobby beamed like the evening star. I felt a lot better. It had been a big burden to me, but it was finally over. All those votes were a catharsis. After hearing the evidence, I knew he probably didn't remember. I must have been one of many. But when I heard him say, "She knows she wanted it," I knew he'd raped her, because that was exactly what he'd said to me.

The judge asked, "Madam Foreman, have you reached a verdict?"

I stood and said, "Guilty, your honor," and winked at Bobby Williamson.

For a while, I toyed with writing horror.

LETTER TO CHARLIE

Dear Charlie,

In 1932, Joe McMurphy was the only survivor of an incident or series of events that caused the demise of his family and his farm animals. And then the family dog killed him. A neighbor, assuming the dog was mad, shot the dog.

No one knows for sure what happened at the McMurphy farm, but it started several weeks prior to the deaths of everyone. I remember hearing about it. I was just a small boy at the time and didn't comprehend what was going on, but people talked about the McMurphy Mystery for years—and later I came to understand.

They say that each of the animals' bodies looked as if it had been slammed or thrown up against the railing or fencing with such force as to kill it, the bones crushed into little pieces. Most of the animals were bleeding from the mouth. All of them had their eyes open—a glazed look across them, as if stunned or shocked, even the chickens. Oh, this wasn't just the animals, I forgot, it was the people too—except old Joe—the dog killed him by mauling him to death... and then a neighbor killed the dog, shot it, thinking it was mad. Not that the dog could have told anyone what happened anyway.

Most of the children's bodies had been crushed against their bedroom walls—little Molly was only six. There was blood splattered across the flowered wallpaper.

One of the kids, I don't remember which one, died on the stairs. He was clinging to the handrail with a look of surprise on his face when they found him, his body like a mass of jelly in his pajamas.

Mrs. McMurphy's body was in the kitchen.

The neighbors thought it happened rather early in the morning and that she was up cooking breakfast for the family—a cast iron skillet was still on the stove with eggs burned to a crisp when they found her. The table was set with plates and knives and forks and napkins, and orange juice had already been poured into juice glasses next to each plate; buttered toast was piled high on a saucer in the middle of the table.

Once, I heard Mother tell someone she thought that Mr. McMurphy had gone out to the barn to milk the cows, or else had heard a commotion and ran to the barn to see what the matter was. No one was sure what time it all was because it wasn't until the neighbor came along and saw the dog hovering around Mr. McMurphy's body—and shot him—that anyone knew what had happened.

I was little, but I heard about it all later as I grew up. I asked Mother if she didn't think it could happen again to us or somebody else, but she said no, and if so, it wouldn't be for years and years, so not to worry about it.

If the newspaper office hadn't burned down a long time ago, I would have looked it up in the old newspaper records to show Jean because she didn't believe me when I told her...

They say that some of the old-timers recall that prior to the incident Mr. McMurphy was at the general store complaining that his animals seemed agitated, but every time he went to the barn, he couldn't find anything wrong, and that there'd been some kind of trouble in town with one of the older kids, but no one could remember what.

Last week, Sally came home complaining that when she was walking downtown to the five and dime, someone pushed her—at least she felt a hard shove at her back, but when she turned around no one was there. It scared her. She was telling Jean about it in the kitchen when I got home. I didn't think much about it at the time, just the wild imaginings of a young girl.

I haven't been sleeping well lately, Charlie, and this morning I heard a commotion outside—sounded like it was coming from the direction of the barn—the chickens were squawking and the cows were crying out and it was so loud that it woke me and Danny Boy up, and of course I didn't go outside where I heard it because we didn't rebuild the barn. We had it torn down because it was in such a state of disrepair.

Instead, I looked out the front door and when I didn't see anything, I tried to call someone, but the lines were dead. I tried to start the pickup, so I could go get help, or take the family with me out of here, I wouldn't want to leave them to face this alone, and then when I realized it was useless, I tiptoed in here and decided I'd write down everything I could remember about the McMurphy incident.

Before we moved back here, I told Jean, we shouldn't buy the place, but she thought there had to be a logical explanation for what happened to the McMurphy family, and you know how she is, there's no arguing with her once she's made up her mind. Besides, she loves the place. She always said it was so quaint and quiet that it would be ideal for her writing, and you know how she loves to fix things up. She's fully restored the kitchen now. I imagine it looks just the same as it did in 1932.

Well, friend, the noise is getting louder, and it's almost daylight—you should see the sunrise in the country, it's really something—anyway, I'm going outside in a few minutes with Danny Boy to see if we can find out what's going on. He's ready to find something, his barking hasn't quit since before I got up

RETRIBUTION

When there was light enough to see, I slipped off my flats and tiptoed along the trail of blood until I found him crouched behind a dumpster. The garbage around him was foul-smelling, though a sweet scent, from his blood, wafted in the air as I grew near. For a moment, I thought I could taste it, until I realized I had bitten through my lip and the bittersweet juice was my own.

I stood behind his cowering figure. Remembering our history, and the things he'd done to other women as well, pity didn't reside in me. His hands were cupped between his legs, his head tucked between his knees. I grabbed a handful of his coarse, black hair and yanked his head back toward me. His white throat bobbed with every moan of fear. I looked down his torso to the patch of dark red saturating his pants legs and pooling beneath him.

The morning light glinted off my straight razor as the first ear flopped to the ground. Once more and no longer would he listen for a woman's steps.

My blade encircled his eyes and with a flick of my wrist no longer would he wait and watch for a female form in the night.

Finally, as I smiled down at his tightly closed eyes and a face twisted in pain, I drew a thin—but ever gaping—red line across his throat. Pleased with my work, I walked out of the alley, ready to face the consequences.

Nonfiction

I originally began research on this piece for my Murdered Judges book. (Murdered Judges of the 20th Century, Eakin Press, 2003) About halfway through the research, I realized Godbee hadn't been a real judge and made the decision to omit this story from the book. I found Edna's story, the whole tale in fact, worth telling, as a part of history, illustrative of how society operated more than a century ago.

MISS EDNA

In 1887, Walter S. Godbee had already been married once and become a widower. The second time around he wanted to make a fresh start, and he wanted to make it with money. Leaving his hometown of Waynesboro, Georgia, he set out to find himself a rich wife whose assets would provide him everything his heart had ever desired.

Perkins, Georgia, so named for the Perkins family, was just up the road a bit from Waynesboro, and seven miles from Millen. Walter, of course, had heard of the Perkins' who owned a bit of everything in those parts. Simeon Perkins and his brother, Shepard, had founded Perkins and Brother, which included Perkins Manufacturing Company in Augusta, Perkins Lumber, and what is now known as Georgia Ironworks.

When Walter arrived in Perkins, he told everyone he aimed to marry the richest girl in the county. And that is precisely what he did.

Born in 1869 in Perkins, Burke County, Georgia, Edna Perkins was the eldest of ten children from the marriage of Simeon Mills Perkins and Mary Tallulah Calhoun Perkins. By the time Walter came upon the scene, Simeon Perkins had passed on to his just rewards in 1886 and had left an estate valued at over $55,000.00 [more than a million and a half dollars in the current economy]. In addition to the corporations, he had owned 3,000 acres in Burke County and a large amount of stock in two railroads.

There was a two-story building at Perkins Junction [as it was called at that time] that Simeon had operated as a general store and post office. When the administrators of his estate decided to close it down, Walter S. Godbee, from Waynesboro, purchased the stock and leased the premises. Though he had no money, Godbee borrowed to finance his mercantile business and made himself postmaster, too. That is how he became well acquainted with the Perkins family and began to court seventeen-year-old Edna. After a few months, they married in July of 1887. Many believe that had Simeon Perkins still been alive, the union between Edna and Walter would never have been. But Edna did marry Walter and, over the course of several years, she bore him three children — two boys, and a girl who the press later dubbed "Sad-Eyed Sarah."

The title "Judge" had been bestowed upon Walter as a title of honor, like many southern gentlemen had been called "Colonel" in earlier times. Walter had worn the title proudly when he arrived in town, dishonoring it later with his treatment of Edna.

Right after the marriage of Walter and Edna, Walter decided it was his duty and his position to manage his wife's father's estate. It was the practice, and, indeed, the law, in previous times, including the earlier part of last century, for women to manage their own estates as long as they were a feme sole. At the moment of marriage, though, the husband became the last word on the management and disposition of property. This was true in the state of Georgia. And it was true in the Godbee family. Being a trusting soul, Edna handed over her assets without giving it much thought.

Walter also gained control over his mother-in-law, Mrs. Perkins' interest. He hadn't done such a great job on his own estate in Waynesboro, and within a short time of his interfering in the Perkins' there was trouble over it in the family. He lost Mrs. Perkins' confidence and became so estranged that though Edna was pregnant, he forbade her to visit her mother. On one occasion, Edna came to discover some mail in the pocket of Walter's clothing. It was addressed to Mrs. Perkins from a cousin who Walter didn't get along with and, apparently, Walter had no intention of sending it to Mrs. Perkins. Edna demanded to know why Walter had not delivered the mail to her mother.

Edna later testified, "He attempted to take these letters from me and in doing so he slapped my face. He bruised my eye and choked me so forcibly that the prints of his fingers were left on my throat, but he got the letters. Finally he did say that he was sorry that he let his temper get away with him to the extent of hurting me and promised me in the presence of my uncle that if I would not leave that he would never hurt me again." A son was born within two months of the incident.

Things progressed peacefully for a while, but when Edna's mother died in 1889, over Edna's protests, Walter insisted upon administering her mother's estate. Again Walter caused dissension in the family and refused to allow Edna to see anyone.

David, the oldest brother in the Perkins family, probably resented Walter the most. He challenged Walter's control over the Perkins' store property. David wanted to start his own business. They became bitter enemies and had a horrible argument in Walter's office later that year, on December 17th. David threatened Walter. The next day when David approached the store, Walter told him not to come any closer, but when David continued, Walter shot and killed him. Family members refuted Walter's story. They remembered it another way, that Walter shot David in the back.

Walter refused to let Edna go to David's funeral or to let her see any of her relatives. She was virtually a prisoner. Two weeks later, the second son was born.

Walter was charged with murder, but claimed he shot David in self-defense. He was having financial problems, because the money he had borrowed to establish his business in Perkins had become due and he couldn't pay both that and a lawyer. Edna still believed in Walter. She loaned Walter the money for a lawyer. The records show that Walter was acquitted, though some members of the family say that no one wanted the Perkins' family dirty laundry aired in public, so the Perkins' family took it easy on Walter.

Things seemed to go smoothly for the Godbees for a while, though they still had financial problems. In 1893, Sarah was born. The business was about to collapse in 1896, and Miss Edna financed their move from Perkins to Millen with another loan to Walter, this time for $2,000.00.

Walter opened another general store, but within a year or so Walter failed again. He then persuaded her to purchase a hotel in Millen to supplement the $300 per year farm income. Edna advanced $2,500.00 from a recent settlement from Perkins Manufacturing. They lived in the hotel for about a year when marital troubles popped up again. Walter set up Edna as the butt of a scandal by arranging for a soldier to stay with her and little Sarah while he went out, but then Walter burst into their rooms and accused Edna of "improper relations." He summoned several people, including his Waynesboro lawyer, and had the soldier arrested. The next morning the soldier was released. For Edna, though, the nightmare hadn't ended. Walter told her that he would file for custody of the children if she didn't sign over the hotel as well as make him sole trustee of her father's plantation. His attorney from Waynesboro had already made out the papers. Edna signed them, but Walter then evicted her from the hotel.

Edna went to Perkins. The children took the afternoon train and joined her. Shortly thereafter, one of Walter's cousins assisted in reconciliation.

Edna returned to Millen on Walter's terms, which included her working for him in the hotel for $10.00 per month, the same salary as a housekeeper. He wouldn't give her any money to make purchases, and a few months later, the hotel burned to the ground [not long after it was fully insured].

Walter and Edna rented a house. Later Edna purchased it with funds from the sale of two Augusta lots she had received from Perkins Manufacturing Company. Edna resented having to continuously use her own funds for the main support of the family and thought Walter should buy her a house. She paid the taxes and insurance, as well as the purchase price, and it was a house she didn't want. This made her feel even more degraded.

Conditions continued to deteriorate when Walter began to openly have extramarital affairs to further manipulate and humiliate Edna. He was doing it partly to restrict her movement and to punish her when she was disobedient. Edna described it as "trouble on account of a colored woman," though Walter didn't limit his activities only to the "high yellows." Walter hated Edna's family. When she visited relatives in Perkins, he would bring "Gertrude" into the house to stay, make Edna's servants leave, and keep Gertrude until Edna returned. Often, he would refuse to let Edna take the children on the visits with her and would send her messages to get her to come home, such as that the children were sick. Upon her return, Edna would discover that he had told deliberate falsehoods.

Gertrude was "set up" in a house Walter owned. Walter hired Gertrude "to cook," and Edna could not get her out of the house. One day, when Walter went off on a short trip, Edna made Gertrude move out of Walter's house, but when he returned, he gave Gertrude his horse and wagon and moved her back into his house. One of the affidavits filed later stated also, that once when Edna was ill, Walter moved Edna out of their bed, brought Gertrude in, and had intercourse with her.

The violence grew worse. Among other things, Walter was a morphine addict. One night, Edna woke up and found Walter standing over her with a gun pointed at her. Both Edna and the children feared for their lives. Edna often left Walter but always reconciled. Walter verbally and physically abused her in front of the children. "He would strike me, slap me, pull me around and accuse me in every way he could . . . of things that were terrible in the presence of my children."

In 1901 they were legally separated, but in 1904 they reconciled again, although both sons argued against it, as did her relatives. Shortly thereafter, Walter promised Edna the good life if only she would agree to move to Atlanta. So the family packed everything up and relocated their household, only to find out that nothing had changed. Their financial situation was still unstable, and Walter was as mean as ever. Edna soon borrowed the money to return to Millen. Although Walter threatened divorce, when she didn't acquiesce and stay in Atlanta, he accompanied her back to Millen.

A month later Edna finally concluded that her only salvation would be to make a final separation. Walter had become more dependent on morphine and threatened "day after day to kill me," Edna testified. He didn't restrict his verbal abusiveness to the home either. Often, he cursed, insulted, and threatened her on the city's public streets.

Finally, she filed for divorce on the ground of cruelty. The divorce was granted in 1908, but Miss Edna came out on the short end of the property division. One of the things she was awarded was a farm, but the lady had to use her small funds to hire someone to run it for her. Eventually, she became so destitute she moved to Augusta and bought a boarding house. She and the children lived there while Walter, who came away from the marriage a big property owner, continued to terrorize her. Before long, he told the boarders that she was a loose, immoral woman and ran a house of ill repute, and drove them away. He succeeded in forcing Miss Edna and the children to return to Millen.

Walter remarried and brought Florence, his new bride, to Millen, to the humiliation of Edna and the entire Perkins family. He also used Edna's money and property to acquire a row of buildings. He not only called them the "Godbee" buildings, but plastered his name across them in large, bold letters, flaunting his wealth and further demeaning the Perkins family.

In an effort to drive her out of Millen, Walter continued to threaten Edna through Sarah. He harassed her and tormented her relentlessly. He would ride by her house four or five times a day. "On moonlight nights, he and Florence would stroll by two or three times." Instead of leaving Millen, Edna bought a .32 caliber Smith and Wesson five-shot pistol and took to carrying it in her bag for protection in case Walter should attempt to do her additional bodily harm.

Walter's new wife, Florence became pregnant. Walter paraded her around town on his arm as if to show the townspeople his new trophy. Each morning Walter and Florence would walk to the post office to fetch their mail. According to her testimony, one morning Edna, now forty-four years old, carrying her white parasol, white drawstring bag, and dressed in a white frock over white lace-up boots, stood at a counter as she wrote out some last minute instructions for Sarah's dressmaker before Sarah and she departed for vacation. As she wrote, she was interrupted by the arrival of Walter and Florence. To Edna, Walter's behavior felt threatening.

"You old whore," Walter muttered under his breath and turned with his wife to leave.

Edna later stated that she feared he would shoot her or hurt her in some way. During the trial, she testified that she remembered pulling open her purse, withdrawing the pistol, and shooting him. The next thing she recalled was that the gun would not fire any longer. Placing the gun back into her purse, Miss Edna lifted up her skirts, departed the post office, and walked back toward her home.

Witnesses and others believe that Edna deliberately entered the post office knowing what time Walter and Florence went there each day. Supposedly Edna's intention was to kill Florence. When she got out the gun, Walter reportedly jumped in front of Florence, took two bullets, and fell down dead. Edna, in a blind rage, continued to shoot the gun until it was empty.

A short time later, the sheriff came knocking at Miss Edna's home. "My God, oh my God, Miss Edna, what have you done!" he cried when she answered the door.

Edna surrendered herself and her pistol to the sheriff.

"I am afraid I will have to take you into custody, Ma'am," the sheriff said, offering his arm.

"I'll be coming with you, Sheriff," Miss Edna replied, linking her arm in his. As they stepped outside into the sunshine, Miss Edna opened her parasol and allowed the sheriff to escort her through the town to the jail. On their way there, one of Miss Edna's boots became unlaced. Miss Edna daintily pulled up her skirts a mite, put her foot on the curb, and permitted the sheriff to kneel down and tie it for her. The remainder of the trip to the jail was uneventful.

Upon her arrival, Miss Edna was allowed her pick of the cells, for it would not do for anyone to say that the town had not been hospitable to a Perkins. She chose the hanging cell because it was the largest. She was not allowed bail, but in a matter of days, there were curtains at the windows and furnishings provided to assure that she would feel at home. After all, a lady of her stature should not be uncomfortable. Of course, she also had a waiting girl with her to take care of her needs.

Walter and Florence were put on a train to Waynesboro, Georgia, where they were buried.

Experts have said the trial of Edna Perkins Godbee convened too near the time of the incident for Edna to receive a fair trial, especially since the prosecution chose to try the murder of Florence Godbee first. It would have been difficult to find a jury to sit on the case of the murder of Walter S. Godbee since his abuse of Edna was so well known. Even though Walter had some friends in what was by then Jenkins County, [Burke and three others having been combined] everyone in Millen knew what lay behind their troubles. Add to that the fact that Miss Edna was a Perkins. And that Walter was much hated in Perkins, Georgia. While it was unheard of for a woman to do such a thing as Miss Edna had done, no one thought what had happened to Walter was undeserved. Some even thought that had Florence not been pregnant, there would never have been a trial at all.

The heinous nature of the other crime, the murder of a woman and her unborn child, was different though. There was a great deal of hostility in the community. The press made wild speculations that didn't help the public cool its heels. Finally, twelve good men and true were seated, for those were the days when women hadn't won the vote, much less the right to sit in judgment in a courtroom.

During the trial, "Sad-Eyed Sarah" visited her mother daily and often lived with her under the executioner's trap door. The press dubbed the girl with that moniker because of the sympathy her pitiful expression evoked each time she arrived at her mother's cell. The trial continued for weeks. Deliberations seemed to take even longer. Finally, the jury returned a verdict. Miss Edna Perkins Godbee had been found guilty. Her punishment was a life sentence in the penitentiary.

Edna bore up as best she could under adverse conditions. She was transported to the prison, where the warden housed her on his premises for the duration. Her only hope was a pardon from the governor, but the sitting governor was not sympathetic to her cause.

Documentation shows that a few years after the trial, Jenkins County residents and others throughout Georgia calmed down enough to see Edna as the victim that she was. An annual letter writing campaign by citizens all over the state, the likes of which had never been seen before, [engineered in a large part by Sarah] supported Edna's parole. Finally, in 1920, she was released.

Some say that Edna's aunt's husband, a well-known senator, decided to make a run for governor of Georgia so that he could pardon poor Miss Edna. As soon as he took office, that's exactly what he did.

"Sad-Eyed Sarah" took her mother in to live with her in Atlanta, far enough away to be well rid of all the gossip. Later, they moved to New York, then Kansas, where Miss Edna lived out her days without ever remarrying. She died in 1931. Miss Edna still has relatives in Perkins, Georgia, as well as elsewhere in the country. But if approached with questions about this part of the family history, the subject would not be open for discussion.

I wrote this piece many years ago while I was still on the bench. When I decided not to run for election for a fourth term, people were baffled. Why? You're a good judge, they said. Why? I believe what I've written in this "true" essay answers that question.

WHY DO THEY STAY? A RHETORICAL QUESTION

A stooped, white-haired old woman, wearing a shirtwaist dress, inches her way to the witness stand with her cane for support. The bailiff assists her as she mounts the first step, the second, and eases into the chair. She puts her mouth close to the microphone and stares through thick glasses at the suited, middle-aged man at her counsel table. Next to him sits a woman young enough to be her daughter, approximately my own age.

At the other table, three men. An old man in coveralls worn over a pressed blue work-shirt, a younger man in a sport shirt, and another middle-aged attorney have been quietly watching the old woman. This is family court. The woman has filed for divorce after fifty-six years of marriage. Before her attorney called her to the witness stand, there had been a lot of paper shuffling. Each side scribbled and whispered amongst themselves for several minutes, after which, the lawyers announced an agreement.

I am the family court judge in Galveston, Texas, an island fifty miles south of Houston. For twelve years, I have heard nothing but divorce, child custody, child support, family violence, child abuse and neglect, adoption, and juvenile delinquency cases. Lately, I don't think I can take it anymore.

After she is settled, the wife stares everywhere but at her husband. I watch her and think that she could be my mother. They are about the same age. This couple has been married about the same length of time as my parents.

After an announcement of ready, I administer the oath to both parties. Her attorney asks the wife to state her name. "Mrs. Foster,"** she says, gripping the microphone like a lifeline. That sounds familiar so I glance through the file in search of something that will answer a question now formed in my mind. I think there is a street by the same name in one of the smaller towns in our county, named after a prominent family. Was it she who coordinated a Christmas food bank one year where I volunteered?

Testifying to the agreement takes five minutes. Her lawyer's voice drones on as he covers the legal requirements for divorce in the state of Texas, then the terms of the agreement. Next, the husband's attorney asks her a few questions. Her turn is over. When I say step down, she looks at me through blank, staring eyes. As her husband gets up from his table, she appears to be trying to hurry toward her own, yet an eighty-year-old woman's hurrying is like that of a wounded eagle. With dignity, she dodges him, haltingly but as quickly as she can. She stares past him, her eyes fixed on some object in the back of the room. When she reaches the nearest chair at her table, she sits down. The younger woman pats her hand.

** **All names have been changed for security and confidentiality.**

The husband steps up to the stand. His attorney elicits testimony. I look at the husband's leathered face as he speaks not a few feet from where I sit. "I don't want the divorce, but if she wants it then I'll sign the agreement." His pate reflects the fluorescent light. His features are faded like worn out clothes. He looks from his lawyer to his wife and back again. She doesn't glance his way.

The attorneys stand. One says, "The paperwork is not quite complete, Your Honor. We reached the agreement at the courthouse steps, so to speak, and have been interlineating changes. There are a few more." After everyone signs, the old woman's lawyer, Ronny, will bring the decree into chambers for my signature. I look from the old husband to the old wife. I wonder, again, why they are divorcing. With no-fault divorce, no one has to say. I briefly remember another case I once heard. The woman couldn't get out of bed. Her family had her brought to the courthouse on a gurney. I heard her testimony in the hall. Terminally ill, she didn't want his name on her gravestone. I wonder whether this old woman now feels the same. I pronounce them divorced, pick up the file, and make my escape.

Busying myself with signing papers that have come up from the clerk, I push the old couple from my mind. I don't want to think about them. It is not good to think about them, to take these things to heart, to take them home. When I'm through, I log onto the computer and check my email.

A light tapping on my door's frame distracts me. The wife's attorney's head juts in. Ronny grips a handful of paper. I roll my chair away from the computer and look up at him.

"All through?"

He tenders the decree and other legal documents. There are, of course, no minor children, but the provisions for division of property fill many pages.

I ask, "Are they the people I think they are?" He says yes. "And were those their children in the courtroom?" Niece and nephew.

Children stayed out of it. I nod. All changes are initialed. Four signatures fill the lines below where I am to sign. I date it, sign it, and place it in the file. "I'll send it down to the clerk." He turns to go. "Wait," I say. "I feel so sad seeing this old couple get divorced after all these years. What happened? Can you tell me? Would your client mind if I knew why?"

Ronny turns in the doorway. I have known this jovial fellow for many years. When I practiced law, we once opposed each other in a nasty trial where the jury deliberated for two days. We spent so many hours together that week that we became friends. Ronny takes a small jaunty step and grins like a boy, but I know his demeanor is a façade. The happy expression doesn't ring true. I know him that well. He shrugs and turns back toward the door. Over his shoulder, he says, "Mrs. Foster's not sad about the divorce. He beat her nearly every day for fifty-six-years."

Why did she stay? Was she afraid to leave? Or was it because her husband held a prominent position in the community, and she didn't think anyone would believe her? When she was young, did she think she could not raise the children alone? Or was it because back when the beatings began, family violence was a dark, ugly secret no one made public? Perhaps she had no job skills fifty years ago and would have had no financial resources.

On the Wednesday of Thanksgiving week, I always let staff go early, to do last minute shopping, to chop the vegetables, to start the fixings for the following day. The courthouse always closes for the Thanksgiving holiday for two days. I am about to tell them to leave. It's after lunch. I am standing in the outer office, chatting with my court coordinator and my court reporter. We are all in good moods. Four straight days off. We are about to leave when Mary, a well-known lawyer, appears in my office, breathless and wide-eyed. "I ran up the stairs to catch you," she says. Behind her is another woman who looks vaguely familiar, though I can't place her.

"Are you about to lock-up?" Mary asks.

I nod. "But if you have a matter for the court, I'll stay." I tell the staff to pack up and go.

She has a counter-petition for divorce and a temporary restraining order. Permission to come into chambers and explain it? She's been to the clerk's office. The clerk will bring the file.

We go into chambers. She introduces me to Krista, her client, whose suit is wrinkled. Krista's appearance is somehow a bit off. No makeup. Hair mussed. Demeanor that reminds me of a yoga position, Downward Facing Dog. I tell them to sit. The client sits. The attorney paces. "Do you recognize my client?" Mary asks. "She used to practice law in our firm, though not family law." Krista never came into my court, Mary says. She got married and quit the firm. She agreed to stay home and raise the children. Her husband is from a very wealthy family. They live in an exclusive subdivision. His father is very influential in Houston.

Krista has three children, aged four, two, and one, a babe in arms. She is unhappy in the marriage. Her husband is possessive, controlling. He doesn't want her to have friends, to go out. He dictates what she is to do each day. She isn't supposed to see her family. She can't work. "To be perfectly honest," Mary says. "He hits her. He hits her if she doesn't do what he says. Not all the time. But it is growing worse." She needs to leave. She needs to get a job. She told him she is going to go back to the practice of law, that she is unhappy. Perhaps if she gets a job, they will get along better. That's what she has told him. But what she meant was that if she went back to practicing law, she could take the children and get away. He wouldn't be able to hit her anymore. She would be safe. Mary says, "But until she gets a job, she has no money. No way to support the children. He controls everything."

Krista has been job hunting. She obtained some interviews. She was hopeful. She returned home the day before and couldn't get into the house. Her key wouldn't work. She thought it was the wrong key. She scrutinized it. It was the correct key. She tried again. She rang the doorbell. She knocked. No one came to the door. She walked around to the backyard gate and found it locked. She called on her cell phone. He answered. "Go away. You can't come in. This is my house."

Krista hitched up her skirt and climbed over the fence. She ran to the patio door, which was locked. She peered through the glass. On the other side, her husband looked at her, an ugly curl to his lip. The four-year-old stood gripping the leg of his father's pants. Her husband held the two-year-old by the hand on his other side. The baby, her husband clutched in his arms.

"Let me in. Please let me in," she pleaded.

"No. This is no longer your house. You want to practice law? Go practice law. You have to leave the children."

The two-year-old is crying. Reaching for his mother. He tries to pull his hand away from his father's. His father restrains him.

"Let me in. You can't keep me from my children. You can't keep me out of my house. This is my house, too."

He tells her to leave. He has a lawyer. His lawyer filed papers. She cannot come into the house. It is no longer her house. If she doesn't leave, he will call the police. She will be arrested. She will go to jail.

She wants her children. "You can't do this to me. I did nothing wrong. You can't keep me out of my own house," Krista says, tears streaming. "It's my house, too. They are my children, too."

"You gave up your children when you started looking for a job," he says. "These are my children. Go away. Go practice law. Leave us alone. We don't want you anymore." He walks to the phone. He drops the two-year-old's hand and begins to punch numbers into the phone. The two-year-old runs to the glass. His face leaves a smear as he tries to claw his way to her. Her handprints blur the other side. The four-year-old throws himself to the floor, crying. The baby wails. She can hear them through the glass. She can see their faces. They are scared. She is scared.

Minutes go by. She screams and cries and begs. He won't let her in. He disappears for a few moments and returns with two uniformed men who follow him into the room. They squeeze through a small opening in the patio door and hand her papers. They are a divorce petition and temporary restraining order. She stands firm and reads the papers through blurred eyes. Her husband looks out on the other side of the glass door. With her peripheral vision, she can see his reflection, his angry face, their children. The temporary restraining order doesn't say she can't go into the house, she tells the two men. The deputy constables say she must leave. There is a hearing in two weeks. She can ask to see the children then. If she doesn't leave, they will arrest her. They will charge her with criminal trespass.

She sees it will do no good to argue. But she has no clothes. No money. Where will she go? They tell her they cannot help her. Will she leave or will they have to take her away? She tells them that she is an attorney. She knows her rights. But she also knows that her husband and his father are very powerful people. She knows if she doesn't leave, they will charge her with as many things as they can. She may never get her children back. She must leave. She gives them one last glance, her family, and climbs back over the fence to her car.

After she drives away, she calls the only person she can think of who might be able to help her get her children back. It is Mary, the attorney in my office now with her, who she worked with before she got married, before she had babies. She found a place to stay overnight. She has worn those clothes two days in a row. It is Thanksgiving tomorrow. She wants to see her children.

The clerk brings the file. I read the order I signed a few days earlier. It is an ordinary petition with a request for a temporary restraining order. Nothing alleged therein calls for her to be barred from the home. I did not sign a kick-out order. I did not order her out of the house or barred from entry. He kept her out illegally. He changed the locks. It is not unusual, but it is not legal. It is not the first time, and it won't be the last time. I feel responsible for this woman's misery, though I only did my job.

"Look at who the attorney is," Mary says.

"I consulted with him," Krista, the mother-client-attorney, says. "I called him weeks and weeks ago and asked him to represent me. He gave me advice. Now he is representing my husband. Am I not right that he can't do that?" The words are argumentative, but the delivery is plaintive.

She is right. He is not supposed to do that. He is a renowned attorney in Houston, an educator, an author of family law books, an authority on family law, and a frequent speaker. He knows he is not supposed to do that, but unless someone files a complaint, nothing will ever be done. Nothing may come of it anyway. He is a powerful attorney.

"What can we do?" Mary asks. I am still reading the papers, first his, now hers. I am reading Krista's affidavit. "Did he really do all these things to you?" Yes, she answers as she bows her head.

I feel sick to my stomach. I tell Mary to call the other lawyer. "Call him right now on my phone and tell him you're here. Tell him I said they illegally restrained this woman from going into her home, they illegally kept her from her children, and that if they don't agree to let her in immediately, I will rescind the entire restraining order."

"Call him? Use your phone?" Mary is again wide-eyed. I recite the number listed on the divorce petition. She stands next to my desk and makes the call.

I am sitting at my signing table with Krista. My small irritation at being kept late on the day before a holiday evaporated moments after the two women entered my chambers. We face each other. Her hair is askew. Her face is blanched and taut as though stretched over a frame. She is very proper, her hands folded in her lap. I glance back at her face. She looks dehydrated, as if she is all cried out. We hear Mary make contact. We watch and listen.

She covers the phone with her hand. "He's not there," she says. "They're going to let me talk to an associate." She waits. Speaking into the phone, she says that she is in the judge's chambers. She tells the person what I said. It takes a few minutes. Asking for my chambers' phone number, she recites it into the telephone. She hangs up. It was the female associate who brought the papers down originally. She is going to call her client and tell him they must come to an agreement.

We wait several minutes. They both say more about the big-name attorney who said to lock her out. They do that all the time in Harris County, they tell me. The judges there let them do it. Nothing ever happens to the lawyers who do it there.

I have heard these stories before, but what can I do except not let it happen in my court? Krista says, "I would have had a hard time believing that a reputable attorney would do such a thing, except now that I'm married into that family, I see things I never would have believed." She clutches her middle. "I don't want to lose my children," she says again.

The phone rings. I tell Mary to answer it. She picks it up and nods. It is the other lawyer. She nods again. Puts her hand over the phone. Whispers. He's agreed.

"Oh, thank God," Krista says.

A few weeks later, I am signing orders and decrees in tall stacks of family and juvenile file folders. Some I sign without reading. I recognize the forms. Some I scan. Some I read closely, especially if I recognize the name of certain lawyers. I come to a joint dismissal. It is agreed; both parties and their attorneys have signed it. Krista, the abused lawyer, and her husband have reconciled and wish me to approve their dismissal of the divorce suit. I sigh, remembering what I heard on Thanksgiving eve, and scribble my signature.

Some weeks later, the chief assistant district attorney for family law comes into my office. "Have you heard the news?" What is it this time? A part of me does not want to know. "Do you remember signing a protective order for us on behalf of one of the court clerks?" I vaguely remember, but I don't know her. She works in civil or criminal, not family. It would have been one of the many I sign each week. This time it happened to be for someone who worked in the courthouse.

The attorney says, "It didn't get served on her husband. It came back. The address was no good. He moved before they could get him." She tells me the district attorney's office was waiting for a new address from her when it happened.

"I don't know what you're talking about," I say.

The clerk and her little boy lived in an apartment on the other side of the causeway bridge, on what we call the mainland. Her little boy is two years old. Her sister went over to visit. When it was time for the sister to leave, the clerk picked up her toddler and, carrying him, walked with her sister down the stairs and out to the parking lot to her car. They said their goodbyes and her sister drove away. The clerk climbed the stairs, her son in her arms.

Hit from behind, she stumbled. Her husband had rushed her. He grabbed her. He forced her and their son into the apartment. They struggled. Her husband was bigger. Stronger. Meaner. He beat her, there in front of their son. He strangled her.

After she was dead, her husband carried her body down the stairs and put her into his car. He took their son to his mother's house. Afterward, he drove into Houston and dumped her body. He is now on the run. Her court supervisor is frightened. She had befriended her, given her advice, encouraged her to leave after the beatings. Her supervisor is hiding until they catch him. A terrible thing. The clerks are all in shock, crying and scared. Feeling they should have been able to do something.

I am not shocked. I am sorrowful, but not shocked. I cannot be shocked any more. I passed shocked after my first year on the bench. I thought I had heard it all when I practiced family law for over eight years. But I also did other kinds of law during those years, so my exposure had been limited. Now, after twelve years on the bench, I know I have heard it all. I heard it all a long time ago. I don't want to hear it anymore.

I think about the violence. The sadness. The meanness. I realize that no matter who I am, what I do, programs I start, cases I hear, I cannot help these people. I think about people who would say about the old lady, why did she stay? And the lawyer, why did she go back? And the clerk, why did she leave? If she had stayed, maybe he wouldn't have killed her. Maybe. Maybe she should have stayed and hoped and prayed she would live to be an old lady. Maybe she should have stayed until her child was grown, which must be what the lawyer has chosen to do. The lawyer has given up her law practice, has given up her freedom, her dignity, and lives in fear every day that she might not live to see her children grown. Maybe the lawyer will leave after her children are out of the house. Maybe she'll live to tell the tale. Or perhaps she will stay until her husband is too old and too weak to hit her one more time. And she will be safe at last.

The clerk thought she was safe. She worked at the courthouse. She knew important people. She knew cops and district attorneys and judges. Why did she leave? Because she couldn't live with the violence anymore. In those last minutes, did she wonder whether she should have stayed? Or did she know she had to take a chance, in order to live?

Why do they stay? More to the point, why are they hit?

I've been accused of being in the wrong business, of taking things too much to heart. I admit I'm guilty. Why am I leaving? My broken heart can't take it anymore.

This is just a little piece I wrote in a nonfiction class I took at Split Rock Arts Program a number of years ago.

SHADES OF GRAY

People think that life is fully in living color, but they have been fooled. It's really not any color at all. It's really a lack of color, not white, not black, but gray, as though someone colored over the picture with black and then white and it washed together into a nothingness.

Because that's what happens, you know. People color everything over for their own benefit. Take a child abuser. Wouldn't something like that make any one of us see red? But not the abuser. It's the child's fault, you see. He's colored it over. The baby wouldn't stop crying. The little boy kept interrupting. The girl argued with him. If only none of them had behaved that way, none of this would have happened. It's no big deal, anyway, it was just one time. It wasn't so bad. And it won't happen again . . . as long as they do what they're supposed to do. It's gray, you see. We're not supposed to notice it.

You could look at alcoholism and drug abuse the same way. Sure, it exists. But it's not as bad as you would think. The alcoholics have Alcoholics Anonymous. The drug addicts have Narcotics Anonymous. The people who eat too much have Overeaters

Anonymous. The Gamblers have Gamblers Anonymous. It is of no importance because these twelve step programs are nothing more than gray places in our society, anyway. It's like sweeping all the addicts under the rug with all the other gray matter the broom picks up.

That, of course, doesn't mean the gray matter we have up top, in our heads. Even if it fell out on the floor, you wouldn't be able to sweep it up. Mop it, perhaps, but more than likely, sponge it. And it would hardly be noticeable since there is no real color to it, so it wouldn't matter if you missed a few bits. The only person to whom it would be noticeable would be the one who lost it.

Well, that's partially true. You have to have some before you can miss it. That's why when some people say things like has *So & So lost his mind*? One must answer in the negative. No more than the rest of his family.

There are various shades of gray, in case you didn't know. When a small child tells a story, it is a very light gray, but when his older sibling stories, the color is closer to the ash on a burning cigarette. A newspaper that inaccurately reports a story is the color of faded ink. When a politician tells a story, it is the color of a battleship. When an old person tells a story it is almost colorless, because no one listens to old people anyway. They might tell us something we don't want to hear.

THANK YOU FOR READING!

If you enjoyed reading *Fly Catching*, I would appreciate it if you would help others to enjoy this book, too.

Recommend it. Please help others find this book by recommending it to friends, readers' groups, and discussion boards.

Review it. Please tell other readers why you liked this book by reviewing it online wherever you received your copy, on social media, and your website.

If you do write a review, please send me an email at susan@susanpbaker.com so I can thank you with a personal note.

If you would like to be on my mailing list so you can receive news of upcoming events and publications, go to www.susanpbaker.com.

ACKNOWLEDGEMENTS

I would like to thank Shauna and Chris for asking Scarlet and Grant if they'd like to pose for the cover of *Fly Catching*. And thank you kids for doing such a wonderful job!

ABOUT THE AUTHOR

Susan P. Baker is the author of nine law-related novels, two non-fiction books, and this story collection. A retired Texas judge, she makes her home in Galveston. She has two children and eight grandchildren.

For more about Susan, go to her website www.susanpbaker.com.
Or to Facebook www.facebook.com/legal writer.
Or follow her @Susanpbaker.
You may contact her at Susan@Susanpbaker.com.

www.ingramcontent.com/pod-product-compliance
Lightning Source LLC
LaVergne TN
LVHW010655110826
845149LV00014B/3102
9780998039022